POISON IN PARADISE

by

Jim Shon

Library of Congress Control Number   2020902006
Paperback: 978-1-7338331-2-7
eBook: 978-1-7338331-3-4

HONOLULU, HI 96822
United States

More books available
at
https://hawaiiinsightbooks.com

The Case of the Good Deed
$3.99 – $9.99

The Case of the Rainforest Reunion
$3.99 – $9.99

Poison in Paradise
$3.99 – $9.99

Hawaii Insight Books
Broadening Your Perspective

Popular categories

New Releases

Soon

Mystery

Politics

Useful links

About

Books

Blog

Civic Education

Contact

Contents

Main Characters

Ramsey Bingham - Chair of the Board of the Sandwich Isles Chemical Corp.

Carleton Brent – London based Insurance mogul

Eastland Bridges – a Hawaii State Senator

Mei-Ling Bridges – wife of Senator Eastland Bridges

Flora Garcia – Children affected by possible pollution

Stephani Harrison– Carleton Brent's personal assistant

Betsy Ito – Office Manager for Eastland Bridges

Barbara Lum – TV Reporter

Bobby Martin – State Senator

Randall Ogawa – State Senator, close friend of Helen Tokugawa

Byron Park – Honolulu detective

Michael Robinson – former staff for Bridges, State Representative

Steven Sinclair – private investigator

Helen Tokugawa – Former staff for Eastland Bridges, State Senator

Bill Wilcox – Plantation Forman

Thelma Winters – Native Hawaiian; Chair, Leeward Community Action Coalition

AUTHOR'S PROLOGUE

This novel was written in the 1980's. I was a freshman legislator in Hawaii. The conversations and politics depicted, while fiction, are based on my thoughts, interactions, and experiences. I was trying to understand what it meant to be an elected official in the Aloha State.

It was a time when there were fewer cable channels, and no Internet. Information about government still came from the print media and broadcast news reporters who actually attended public hearings with camera men. Generally, there were many more news people assigned to cover the legislature, and many fewer competing sources.

It was a time when personal relationships were stronger, both among elected officials and between the elected and the voters. Smoking was not yet banned from the capitol. Individual personalities seemed to be larger than life. Sugar and pineapple were still major players in our economy, and in our politics.

My personal perspectives were formed by someone who had worked at the legislature, and just been elected for the first time (after losing twice before).

It is not the novel I would write today. It is a snapshot in time, perhaps before the explosion of information that has so watered down the intensity of the community's relationship with their elected government. It is perhaps not as politically correct as it might be.

All characters and events are fictional, but based on composite observations and experiences with real people I knew in the 1980s. As with all of life, outward appearances can be deceiving. What may seem obvious may turn out the opposite. There is a personal and inner life to politics that deserves our attention. Government, in the end, is made up of individuals with contradictory aspirations, personal thoughts, anxieties and egos.

This manuscript sat in a box for some 25 years. When I dusted it off, I was struck by how many issues raised then are still relevant today. Nothing has been changed from the original, except removing typos and awkward grammar.

In the end I hope it is an enjoyable read, with a bit of insight into our democracy, set in the most beautiful place in the world.

—Jim Shon August 15, 2009

CHAPTER ONE

Ethyl waited in the stale air of the elevator as it slowly rose from the basement of the Hawaii State capitol to the second floor. She stared blankly at the stained carpets and the worn control buttons as she had done hundreds of times before. Fifteen years ago she had felt privileged to ride in the same elevators with important people, engaging in whispered, knowing conversations. Now, she knew better. Her naïveté and excitement had slowly turned to disappointment, then boredom. The slender impatient idealists had gradually gained weight and patience, and inevitably gave up their ideas and ideals. *Life goes on*, she thought.

The elevator stopped and paused before opening its doors, as if to remind passengers that nothing in government could be hurried.

She yanked at the canvas trash container on its metal frame as it stumbled across the gap in the floor for the doors and squeaked out onto the gray stone floor. Still, it was a grand building, she thought. Four square floors surrounding a huge, open atrium, inviting all to an inner courtyard and gathering space. The afternoon sun shone against the polished wooden railing. Her eyes adjusted to the light and automatically surveyed the open court to see who was working, gossiping, or scheming, all of which she had come to regard with equal importance. In the far corner, a couple of staff members from the Senate Judiciary Committee were listening attentively as a former legislator, unable to break cleanly with his memories of glory and power, told them how it was in the good old days. At least that's what she imagined him to be talking about. She reflected on how much fun people-watching had once been for her.

She wheeled the container ahead of her like a shopping cart. As she passed each austere wooden door she casually noted their intimate secrets. *This one serves the best raw fish on opening day; that one keeps scotch in her desk; this one always hires his relatives; that one has a new refrigerator; this one leaves his jogging shoes out – PU!*

Speaking of bad smells, someone had complained about one coming from Senator Bridges' office. *Probably some food left over from a recent party*, she expected. Politics is food, someone once said, and she nodded knowingly while glancing at her expanding waist and not so loosely fitting slacks. Even the maintenance people ate well at the capitol.

Ten feet from the Senator's door her nose detected an unpleasant and unfamiliar offense. *Doesn't smell like fish, or any food for that matter*, she thought. She jangled her keys and was about to unlock the door but noticed it was already unlocked. As she swung it open, the odor practically knocked her over. Nothing seemed amiss in the reception area - only a partly crinkled piece of paper lying just in front of the door. She picked it up and glanced at it absently. FROM THE OFFICES OF PALAKA PRODUCE, INC. read the letterhead. On its face was written "Sen. E. Bridges, Room 201," and a phone number. She shoved it into the trash bag and began to move toward the inner office, and the obvious source of the smell.

At the sight of the partly decomposed body Ethyl screamed and ran into the trash container as she rushed out of the office. She twisted her ankle on the way down the stairs to the security office. One week later, still recuperating, she made up her mind to submit her resignation and never again return to the capitol building.

***

Helen Tokugawa had been an eager high school student when her social studies teacher invited a newly elected state legislator to speak before the class. Representative Eastland Bridges' topic was *Why We Should Care About Politics.* She remembered that he spoke for some time looking at the back wall, as if there existed an imaginary gallery of interested fans, but that he really did look right at them in the question and answer session. He wore an Aloha shirt, Liberty House slacks, and expensive shoes. Helen was ready to write him off as just another preachy adult who was "irrelevant" when she thought of a good question and caught his eye.

It was in 1970, and the big issues were Viet Nam, civil rights, and the local rivalry between Governor John Burns and Lieutenant

Governor Tom Gill. She expected to hear more about one of these when she asked: "What's the most important issue for the people of Hawaii?"

For the first time, Bridges, in her view, expressed true emotion. "The most important issues will be who will run Hawaii and for what purpose? Will it be the big corporations, whose profits are the only standards of action or will it be citizens like you, who represent not an institution but the Islands and the dreams of its people." Bridges was beginning to echo the rhetoric of the day, that combination of emotional nostalgia for things born of Hawaiian culture and the growing desire for self-reliance. In doing so, he began to talk over the heads of some students, no longer making his answers simple, no longer even aware that his audience was young and inexperienced. He was speaking from the heart, and every student understood that what he had to say must be very important.

"And not only must we ask who will rule, we must ask for what purpose. We must decide if we are just going be to another selfish and wealthy class of oppressors, or responsible stewards of the Earth, and brothers to the weak and poor." He paused, and noticed that the whole class was becoming uncomfortable. His words were just a little too strident for young minds insulated from the outside world. Even the teacher was visibly uneasy.

The teacher quickly thanked the Representative, and he left feeling that at least he told them something more than the usual civics bullshit. At least he gave them a glimpse of the real world. The young Eastland Bridges was yet to replace his cutting ideology with the grace and charm of his more mature leadership. For the time being, he only hoped that some of those students knew what he was talking about.

Some did. Helen Tokugawa, impressionable child of the late sixties and its radical rhetoric, self-styled Marxist without knowing what that meant, determined that day that politics could be a noble profession, and that it would be hers.

She began by waving signs and campaigning for Bridges in the next election. In Hawaii it has become a fixture of politics to see office seekers along the side of the road with a large sign, waving at the cars. It was both charming and ridiculous. Just the sort of thing to draw in young people and old alike - a community event, when several dozen or even hundreds gathered at one time. It was Helen's first experience of the gap between lofty purposes and every day, slog-it-out winning of the votes.

She became a student intern at the legislature, and eventually landed a job on Bridges' staff as a researcher for his Senate Health Committee, of which he was its new chairman. Her road to the political life was much like many young staff members. It began with a mild form of hero worship. If they were lucky, they grew beyond such idolatry without losing their optimism. Some never lost the need for the father figure, and only substituted one for another throughout their political careers.

As filled with rhetoric as she was, Helen could not help but be overwhelmed at the sights and smells and postures and formalities of her first days on the job at the capitol. She was not yet a full-fledged staff member. She learned to dress as a young professional, that combination of subservience and eager-to-please polish the government loves to surround itself with. Papers were important. In school, papers were part of everyday small tasks. But here, they were *really* important – they were the weapons in an elaborate and mystifying strategic battle. They affected people's lives. New staff members were given special orientations to show them how to behave, and to familiarize them with the conventional forms used in bill drafting and committee reports. As a newcomer, everything seemed important, and this importance was transferred to make the staff feel, at least at the beginning, that everything they did was absolutely essential to the wellbeing of everyone in Hawaii

Part of the appeal of the capitol was its assembly of cliques and clubs and comrades. The staff members tended to gather and gossip in the galleries during "Session," the daily formal assembly of House and Senate in their own impressive modern chambers. Each circle of new-found friends kept up a constant intelligence network as to who was preparing a special lunch which could be sampled. Most legislators made efforts to integrate themselves with the legislative community by providing *heavy pupus*- an Island euphemism for a wide variety of food ranging from potato chips to catered buffets and drinks. The conflicts and hot tempers, so much a part of each legislative term, were engulfed in the sizzling smoke of Portuguese sausage on an electric grill, and diverted with spicy raw fish specially flown in courtesy of the always gracious neighbor island delegations. At times it was hard to stay angry at legislators and their staffs who were guilty of slighting colleagues, pandering to special interests, or failing to live up to commitments. Helen used to lie awake at night trying to deal with these feelings. Her youthful militancy wanted desperately to sustain a righteous anger; it was so satisfying, so pure. Yet, she was a child of the Islands, and could not completely turn off her love of food, and song, and the gracious aloha which often permeated legislative life.

The hypocrisy, she insisted, and the excitement, she admitted, began with one of the most unusual political rituals in America. Most states celebrated the opening of their legislative terms, but none turned that event into a public extravaganza of food and music and flowers like Hawaii. The capitol became an agitated ant hill with lobbyists, friends, family members, staff, bureaucrats, and tourists forming an undifferentiated colorful stream up and down the cement stairwells, jammed into the elevators, milling through the open halls, office to office, plate lunch to plate lunch. The best connected legislators always had a jovial Hawaiian combo with their ukulele, guitars, bass, and lilting falsetto singers egging on one of the secretaries in a risqué hula. Thousands of invitations to loyal supporters, and anyone who might be of use in the future, had been sent to ensure that every possible member of the political community in Hawaii felt personally welcome. Those modestly active in community affairs would receive a dozen or more combination Christmas - New Years - Opening Day invitation greeting cards or letters each year. These were obviously form letters sent out by staff and campaign workers, and everybody knew it, but felt good about getting them anyway. It was a day to have one's picture taken with an unrecognizable figure piled with so many flower leis that only the nose and eyes would peek out above the crown of honor and admiration. The smell of plumerias, the taste of Japanese hot mustard and raw fish, the texture of macaroni salad smothered in mayonnaise, and the sound of pop-top beer and soda cans made it difficult to believe that somehow this circus was a prelude to serious business.

Helen would have dismissed the whole affair as "bourgeois" were it not for the remarkable collection of people who rubbed elbows on that day. Department heads smiled to the department secretaries they never acknowledged on the job. Lobbyists for condominium developments joked with their environmental opponents. Advocates of every stripe cornered weary Senators and Representatives whose only response might be "call me during the week." Everywhere were the young veterans. They were the experienced staff members, perhaps in their third or fourth or fifth session. Since most staff was hired only for the four-month regular session, departing in hopes to convert their new contacts into permanent jobs, to be able to arrange ones' life to return and apply your experience was rare. A premium was placed on bagging an experienced secretary or researcher for one's staff. On opening day, these treasured workers surveyed the new freshmen legislators as drill sergeants appraising the new recruits. They sought inconspicuous corners and conducted muted discussions of what to expect in the weeks to come, and who might emerge as candidates for leadership in the future. They had a lot to do with what actually got done in this building, but very few ever achieved a position of recognition or power. They lived through their bosses, although the bosses changed. They wrote the bills, fashioned the language of committee reports, did the research and tried to push their elected mentors along the path of their own agendas. Helen could never figure out if they absorbed the atmosphere of the building or created it.

Working at the capitol required a new vocabulary. The most important thing to understand, Helen came to believe, was the idea of TRUST. Trust was a word used by nearly everyone in nearly every situation. As first she thought it simply meant agreement. *Someone you trusted was someone you agreed with.* Then one day, Senator Bridges had told her a particular lobbyist was someone he could trust, the very same man who had been working against what Bridges was for. She adjusted her definition: *trust meant honesty and reliability.* But there was more to it than that.

One Friday, as the sharp afternoon sun made the floor-to-ceiling windowed side of the office uncomfortable, the staff had been gathered in a circle near the door gossiping about how uppity so-and-so's administrative assistant was. Mellowed by those older and wiser, Helen also condescended to add her anecdote of how she too had been snubbed. Eastland Bridges arrived with a huge bag of boiled peanuts – an Island favorite he'd gotten from another legislator. 'That was nice of him" his office manager Betsy offered.

"He's a nice guy to the staff, but I just don't trust him," said Michael, as all five of them pulled up the waste baskets to discard the shells. Michael Robinson was Bridges' most senior and trusted aide, and often affected the certainty about people thought to be a sign of a veteran. The Senator was amused by this judgment, and joined the group after opening the 3-foot high refrigerator to grab one of those small cans of pineapple juice given free to every office by the pineapple lobbyists. "Why do you say that, Michael?"

"He's too independent. Makes a lot of speeches about good government, open government, reforms for this, reforms for that. All talk. I just don't trust him."

"So he's for good government. So he gets votes by talking about it. What's wrong with that?" Bridges was enjoying himself. He leaned back in his chair with that look on his face as if to say, "Here's Socrates, probing the minds of his young students." Michael knew the look, but allowed himself to be used in order to pursue his analysis.

"Opinions are nice to have. What was it that Governor Burns said in the 70 campaign? Any damn fool……"

"So what's the point?" Helen interrupted.

"The point is that you can't tell much about someone just by listening to them. You have to know who they're close to. What groups do they belong to? What their background is. Just because he says he's an environmentalist, for example, that doesn't mean you can count on him in the clutch. If he belongs to the Sierra Club, marches against the development of a valley, testifies against the new H-3 highway, if all the relevant parts of his life say he is an environmentalist, then, maybe…maybe. The question in my mind is always who do we know that he is completely loyal to, and who will give him hell if he messes up? Or to put it more crudely, how do we get to him? Who do we call to reach him? Who does he listen to?"

"Sounds like your idea of trust is my idea of being in somebody's pocket," Helen declared, as she glanced at Bridges for approval. He remained amused and noncommittal as his eyes shifted back to Michael for his defense.

"We're not talking about ethics, or morality. I wish you'd get off that black and white kick. It's a matter of what interest group, what context, what sub-culture, what mind-set you belong to. And everyone, my little Marxist, belongs to *some* interest group."

"Just because I'm not in love with capitalist oppression doesn't make me a Marxist," Helen snapped, aware how childish she was sounding.

"Michael has a point." Bridges began, as the rest of the staff leaned slightly closer to hear what the boss had to say. "Sometimes it is hard to know just where someone is coming from without that background information, and even then, people do change their minds, they do listen to their consciences. I remember the days when being a union man was almost the same as being a Democrat. If you weren't solid on a few issues that the union was interested in, you just couldn't be trusted. There was a litmus test. Another way of putting it was, *Could the union pressure you into keeping your commitment?* The same thing could be said of the Chamber of Commerce types, the big corporations, the community councils, everybody. Then along came Joe Patton, who never got anyone's signature but his own on his proposed bills. Who never got a union endorsement. Who ran on a platform of being totally independent. Lots of people were attracted to him. He made a lot of sense. But you just couldn't predict where he would be on any issue. You just could not count on his vote. Sometimes you got the impression that he'd be insulted if you asked him to commit himself to a group's goals. He was independent on principle, he said. He seemed to treat those who did cooperate and compromise with contempt. We were all corrupt, he often implied. He talked a lot about open government, but he never got a single bill passed. It was Henry Mitsui who pushed through that Sunshine Law. And Henry was never accused of being independent. He as a team player all the way. When the time came for the team to support that bill, it was all the way, not a complaint. And there were plenty in Henry's circle that hated that bill, too. But they went along."

"Are you saying that trust just means joining a group and going along?"

"Life is never that simple." Bridges reflected. "All I'm saying is that in the legislature, what counts are votes. Not *your* vote. Not an individual's vote – but a collective vote. If you don't have the votes, you don't do a damn thing. You're just there to massage your ego. For a citizen who goes to the polls, his or her vote is private, individual, a matter of conscience. But in a public body like this, the real choice is not how to vote on a bill but what group to join, what leader to follow. You can't just stand around and preach on the nobility of public office. You have an obligation to get something done. If you don't like the idea of compromise, you really have no business being a legislator."

Betsy Ito, an attractive 45-year-old widow in her fifth year as an office manager, felt the young members might get the wrong impression. "But there still is room for an individual's conscience, isn't there?" she prompted.

"Just words,' said Michael, trying to sound seasoned.

"Not entirely, Bridges interrupted. Michael was beginning to sound like so many staffers who had absorbed the techniques of government but never really embraced the soul of it. Many legislators started out idealists and slowly adapted to the realities of decision making among 76 people. But these young ones, they were so...so... unprincipled. They began with the harsh reality and never got around to the ideals. Bridges could never decide how he would tell Michael not to run for office. He could see it now. Michael would be hurt, but he would find his own small group and do it anyway. He would get in, but it would never be the same between them. Bridges had seen former staff members elected only to completely ignore their former bosses. Not even talk during caucus. The Michaels in the world would find another mentor, usually with lots of ready-made power and cash to lavish on an eager-beaver freshman, and the rest would be history. It was an inevitable painful future Bridges did not relish. He sensed that Michael also recognized that their teamwork would not last forever.

"Michael, you're too Machiavellian," Bridges chided, trying to hide his distaste for the man's lack of values. "Of course, conscience is always a factor. Even the most loyal members of a group are allowed to deviate, even work against the group, on occasional matters of conscience. The important thing is sincerity. If someone is truly troubled by something, people will understand. All's fair. Do what you have to do. But don't overstate this conscience matter either. There really are very few issues where a person feels so strongly as to justify breaking a commitment, or breaking with a group. Most legislators don't get excited about a wide range of issues. Most don't really feel that principle is involved in every bill. Occasionally - yes, everyday - no. Perhaps it is this recognition that leaves me a bit uneasy when someone stands for principle and conscience every day of the week. Does he really mean it? Is it possible to feel so strongly all the time? I doubt it. Sincerity and conscience are limited resources – finite. They must be used sparingly, appropriately."

"But I've seen you get mad with people who break with your group," Betsy argued. Helen nodded agreement.

"I know it, and sometimes I'm right because they are not sincere, and sometimes I'm just mad because I can't get my way. But what my reaction is doesn't say anything about another person's sincerity. Lots of times it's only after the dust has settled that colleagues can sort out their differences and heal their wounds. You can never wait for smiles of approval before you go out on a limb for your conscience. You better be sure you know what you are doing. It better be worth it. You may end up paying for it anyway."

Trust was definitely something worth thinking more about, Helen concluded. It was a hidden criterion that everyone judged everyone else by. It was the basis of being included, and of being able to make a difference. But how do you join a group you can't respect? I though public life should reflect a certain clarity. Some were the good guys, and some were not. Helen felt uneasy, realizing that her confidence and frame of reference were being eroded, shaken up and redistributed in unfamiliar territory. She began to appreciate the courage, heroism, and sometimes tragedy of public life. *You got praised for stupid things, and condemned for stuff you didn't do.* But as she wrestled with these unsettling thoughts, her determination to make this her life had grown stronger.

If trust was difficult to understand, being bought off with crumbs was something beyond comprehension for Helen. In just her first year as an intern, she had noticed how big a deal some legislators made about which office they got. Among the demeaning, in her view, tasks for young staff members was visiting offices to get signatures on bills and resolutions sponsored by Bridges. Sometimes he would indicate a select few of his colleagues to be sought out. Other times, she would attach a roll call sheet to the manila folder and get as many legislators as she could corner. Just as the genteel trade winds constantly below through the palm trees in Hawaii, the young staffers in search of signatures silently drifted up and down the halls, not sure if their task was important or not.

In spite of her misgivings about the process, Helen had used those opportunities to size up each legislator and their staff. In contrast to her office, where Bridges refused to allow smoking, many offices were filled with cigarette smoke – and most had empty coffee cups, and piles and piles of bills and resolutions being sorted and put into three-ring binders. Large abstract paintings, parceled out by a central state art pool, hung not so much as statements of taste or beauty but as symbols of modern professionalism. Few staffers really liked them.

Since as many as five or six staff members might have to work in close proximity to each other, the size of the office, as well as providing some prestige, was also related to day-to-day comfort. In general, the most powerful got the biggest offices. Some incoming freshman got a first-come, first-served pick, but most were at the discretion of the Speaker or Vice Speaker of the House, or the President of the Senate. A common mistake, Bridges explained, was that freshmen became indebted to leadership just to get a better office, and those debts were later collected on matters of substance. "Never become obligated over something as trivial as an office," Bridges warned.

Helen could identify at least two representatives who "sold their souls" for a better office arrangement. In later years, she would laugh at her once harsh and exaggerated judgment about offices, but as a new underling, she was sure she had put her finger on the pulse of power politics.

In her second year at the capitol, Helen became a full-fledged member of the staff, and was assigned to "cover" the House Finance Committee. There, she had found the real meaning of "crumbs."

The House Finance Committee was made up of its all-powerful, and very experienced Chairman – often the only legislator reverently referred to as simply THE CHAIRMAN; his staff, which usually was more experienced than most of its members; a Vice Chair, waiting in the wings for the Chairman to retire, and a few "safe" and loyal veterans who didn't want the work load associated with being chair of a major committee; and of course, a collection of eager freshman legislators. The freshmen were assigned to Finance presumably since it was a great place to learn all the aspects of government. The real reason, however, was that they would be so overwhelmed with the numbers and the programs that The Chairman would have pretty much a free hand to run things as he, in conjunction with The Speaker, saw fit.

Helen found it was customary for THE CHAIRMAN to say as little as possible, and to affect the air of the quiet and powerful. She recalled reading spy novels where the closer you got to someone of true power and intelligence, the less colorful they became. *Power did not require arguments, or postures, or clever and facile speech. The weaker the man or woman - the greater their need for speeches.* So it was in the state legislature when Helen Tokugawa looked at life through the eyes of newcomer.

"It's a conspiracy of deception," said Bernard authoritatively. Bernard was one of Helen's fellow intern-turned staffers that year. A product of the university's political science department, complete with models and formulas in his head about how the world worked, Bernard had become convinced that the Finance Committee was a snake pit of sinister purposes.

"Let me explain how these things work" he began, leaning over the wooden railing with his long brown hair– a symbol of the casual intellectual he sought to be. "Like most committees, membership is structured to maximize the perpetuation...."

"Bernard," Helen interrupted, "can you for once explain what you mean in plain English? I mean, I love the dialectic, or whatever, but..."

"OK, OK. Every Finance Committee always has the energetic freshmen who's openly declared purpose is to play the role of son or daughter to the affectionate Chairman. They work hard and are always unable to tell the difference between what is important and what is trivial – when it is time to coast and when it is time to focus. They always vote with the Chairmen, and hope for some minor capital improvement for their district. They can always be counted on to support even the sleaziest proposals in the name of innocence and loyalty."

Helen could not, on principle, allow Bernard to express an unchallenged opinion. She enormously enjoyed his sparkling eyes, always so full of intensity and energy. He loved ideas, and models, and all manner of abstracting the world. He created worlds all to himself, and for this alone Helen would always remember with fondness those days when she and Bernard debated the small things in life as if they were profound.

"Bernard, you obviously haven't been sitting in many meetings. In fact, I'm actually impressed with a number of the new guys. They seem to learn fast and ask the kind of questions you know the Chairman would rather they never touched. On the other hand," she quickly added before Bernard could defend himself (she could tell when he was about to because he always lifted his chin and his eyebrows together), "you are right about the lackeys. Except I'd say some of the most loyal and passive ones are the veterans, not the newbies." There was hollowness to her words, for both knew that their opinions were based on only a few impressions early in the legislative session. They knew, to the extent each was honest, that their harsh judgments would need to be revised again and again. Today's apparent dolt may turn out to be a brilliant hero in three months. But Helen did share the frustration and even anger over how Finance seemed to operate.

"I can't believe it. How can they let him treat them that way? It's as if they were children," Helen was ranting as she stormed back into the office one day.

"What have the capitalist dogs done today, comrade Olga," Michael quipped as he stalked past her, not bothering to lift his eyes off a yellow committee report. She ignored his remark and peeked into the inner office to see if Senator Bridges was alone and approachable. He looked up, and having heard some of her outburst, invited her to sit down with a nod of his head.

"What's up?"

"It's Finance again. He's treating them like children. How can they take it sitting down? How can they pretend it's just OK to be treated like children?"

"Calm down. Explain."

"The worksheets, even the private notes, of each member are declared to be secret, privileged, and will not be allowed out of the room. Can you imagine, telling elected officials they cannot take their notes outside? It's just like being in high school. And the ridiculous thing is that the committee members accepted this. How do you explain that?"

'What's there to explain? He doesn't want the House position on specific budget items circulated before they actually go into Conference Committee with the Senate. Merely a security precaution," Bridges stated evenly, pretending that he accepted the excuse.

"Helen, let me tell you what is going on in their heads. They suddenly belong to something few people share. To run for office means you accept a view of yourself that is not humble, but overconfident, an exaggeration of what you can do for people. You survive a year-long, rugged and exhausting campaign. You had to keep going, getting up in the dark to wave at cars, going to meetings, walking to door to door and facing the dogs. You nurture that inner motivational voice: *I'm better than the other guy. I'm going to do a better job.*

"So you finally arrive here, and amid all the kinds of congratulations and leis and a sense of accomplishment. All of a sudden your role has changed. Your job is not to sell yourself on the inside. Your job is to serve. It is a completely different psychological feeling. And not many can easily, or ever, make the transition. Some just never stop campaigning. People just can't flip flop like it meant nothing. Personal pride grows when you arrive. And ironically, you know what feeds pride and feeling you are important? It's being part of an exclusive club, a family, and part of something bigger. You are willing to give up being an individual at times to prove you belong. To be part of something bigger. To be an accepted member. One of the elite. One of the chosen. One of the few citizens who have ever gone through the trial of the campaign. Your own office, your own stationary. Your own staff hired by you and only you. People who are twice your age and make twice your income are forced to defer to you. They have to be polite because they imagine you have power. And how did you get it? Thousands of people gave it to you. No one else can claim that they were "hired" by four, five or six thousand citizens. It is not too much a leap to believe that to honor democracy, to honor the voters, you honor their representative - the new member of the exclusive club. That is representative democracy in all its arrogance and humility, all bundled and twisted together."

Bridges was so absorbed in his words that he'd risen and began pacing up and down, waving his arms. His voice grew strong. His audience became the wall, the ceiling.

"People deal with this intoxication in lots of ways. One is to become a pet of leadership. Whatever you say, goes, big daddy. If I vote for your bill, will you give me a piece of candy? A bigger office? Pass my resolution congratulating Mrs. Wong for winning the biggest tomato contest at the State Fair? Now, they don't call people, they don't visit other offices. No, now you guys come to me. I'm the hot shot now. I don't go across the street to the department. It's their job to genuflect at my altar."

Helen thought, *My God, he's going to have a nervous breakdown.*

Bridges did not have a breakdown. As abruptly as he had risen to his passionate monologue, he sat down and looked silently with curiosity and admiration at his young disciple.

"Helen, you know what keeps me going?" His speech was subdued. "In spite of all I've said, there are still lots of public servants who manage to get a hold of themselves. And who manage to sincerely attempt to serve. In fact, it's a majority. They do their homework. They fight the ego, and believe me it's a daily battle. They try to get back in touch with that part of them that still sees the big picture, and still values humility. I know it's discouraging to see both new and older legislators, people who have spent so much time and effort to get there, just roll over and be ordered about. I wonder what their constituents would think. But some of them will snap out of it. Some will reflect back, and feel regret. Some will come out of it with renewed strength. And in the end, very rarely can one or a few people really manipulate the whole legislature. In the end, peoples' consciences can be felt. You know, almost every day I go down on the floor for Session a get a little tingle. For better or for worse, I'm about to participate in a remarkable drama. Oh, it may not really be dramatic, and a particular day may be boring. But by God it is a democracy. And that's both scary and wonderful."

He noticed that she was staring at him. She noticed that his eyes were watery.

"Now pull yourself together young lady. Be strong. Someday you may be here and getting angry won't solve anything…" After a short pause, he nodded toward the door, and she took the cue and left.

In later years, as she remembered all the times she had been with Bridges, Helen most remembered that afternoon when she was so angry, and he so candid.

CHAPTER TWO

His car glided smoothly out of the dim tunnel and out into the sunlight of windward Oahu. He eyes adjusted quickly as he glimpsed the wall of green, the distant blue ocean, and the shoreline of Kaneohe Bay. He loved to come to this side of the island. It was his relief from the traffic and heat of Honolulu. Even though he seldom drove over more than once or twice a month, it was important to know that there was such a place. It was green, cool, and rural. As he sped past the banana patches on his left he wondered how long even this oasis would last before progress paved it over. Already the traffic was unbearable during rush hour.

He turned left onto Kahekili Highway, named after an ancient Hawaiian Chief, and his mind drifted to the other school mates who were no longer alive. A few had died right after graduation in Viet Nam. Just last year the girl he'd taken to the senior prom had been fatally injured in a car accident on the mainland. At forty-two he was beginning to be aware of his own middle age, and even his own mortality.

He slowed and turned into the Valley of the Temples Memorial Park and followed the narrow driveway as it wound past the well-manicured lawns of the cemetery. He spotted the line of parked vehicles and the crowd of mourners at the gravesite. Late again.

Detective Byron Park edged his way quietly to the back of the crowd, silently paying his last respects to a man he had known as a close friend in high school, but who had drifted apart in later years. He could see several prominent legislators in the front row, along with Eastland's widow Mei-ling. Her two-year-old son was tended by a grandparent. A Hawaiian minister, in his oversized white smock, was conducting a prayer he could not hear.

His eyes wandered to the impressive cliffs far above, covered with green, partly obscured by the clouds they trapped. To his right was an equally beautiful view of the Bay, except this was partly spoiled by commercial development across the highway from the cemetery entrance. He was glad he came.

Eastland Bridges was the last person he'd expected to be putting to rest. Bridges, in good health, and the same age as Park, was a popular politician. Could have been governor one day he suspected, although he never paid that much attention to politics. His death seemed pretty routine. A legislator visits his office to do some work, decides to have a few drinks, trips over a waste basket and hits his head on the edge of the desk. A freak accident. Happens all the time, really, except not to well-known people. More accidents occur at home, he knew. No one missed him for several days. Apparently he was about to leave on a mainland trip and everyone just figured he'd gone as planned. Life sure in unpredictable.

If it had been a truck driver, or a housewife, or a cop like me, there would be little official interest, he thought. *But because he was important, it was necessary to at least go through the motions, ask a few questions, and assure the public and especially the press that nothing was funny. He wished somebody else would have been assigned to this one. Who wants to poke your nose into the private lives of people at a time like this?* He didn't look forward to his mandatory visit to Mei-ling later that day.

The minister concluded his prayer, and first the immediate family, then a number of friends, passed by the coffin and left a flower or two. Helen Tokugawa watched as Michael Robinson tried to control his feelings. Michael was obviously upset. He and Eastland had been at odds with each other ever since Michael had voted for the highway bill in his first term in the House. It was a bitter disappointment to Bridges, but Helen was not surprised. Years ago, before either had been elected, when they both worked for Eastland, she could sense that Michael would follow his own path. Failing to get Bridges' blessing to run for office, he had surprisingly come up with a well-financed campaign to defeat an incumbent. He seemed a rising star. But then his career had stalled. Leadership refused to give him a major committee. By the time Helen had run for the Senate, Michael was still treading water in the House. He was clearly jealous of her. She had been his underling. Now, in her first election, she'd bypassed him right into the Senate. Her old contacts on Bridges' staff had told her of a number of sharp arguments between Michael and Eastland. Yet today all was apparently forgotten. Or perhaps it was guilt, for not living up to his former boss' high standards. Michael was barely able to speak above a whisper. All during the ceremony he had just stared at the ground with his mouth partly open. *Maybe there still is a decent bone in his body*, Helen had conceded.

As she walked back to her car, she nodded to Detective Park, who had visited her yesterday. Helen was not able to provide any information to shed light on Bridges' death, and Park didn't seem to be looking for anything in particular.

Park recognized other mourners. There was Bill Wilcox, foreman at one of the plantations. Park had dealt with Wilcox a few years ago when the prosecutor's office was trying to shut down the cock fights held on plantation property. Wilcox was a large, heavy-set man in his fifties. He moved in two worlds. As a confident of the management, he helped negotiate the stingiest wage agreement with the union, was invited to high class parties where he obviously did not belong, and occasionally helped to lobby for their special bills at the legislature. At the same time, the workers granted him a grudging respect, and even shared many a laugh with him at the local bars. Wilcox was a hard living, hardworking man, totally devoted to plantation agriculture in the Hawaiian Islands. His wife had left him years ago.

Next to Wilcox was Ramsey Bingham, a well-known developer and Chair of the Board of the Sandwich Island Chemical Corporation, which supplied the plantations with fuel and pesticides. No doubt, both of these characters had come to know Bridges in his recent work with the Health Committee. *Funny how rivals become friends in time of death,* Park thought, as he watched Wilcox and Bingham converse just out of earshot.

Before leaving the cemetery, Park strolled over to the Korean-Chinese section. He snapped off a dead leaf from a potted plant next to his grandfather's grave. He had come to Hawaii as a Korean nationalist in 1910. His dream was to return to a free and independent Korea. But the Japanese had turned his homeland into a colony, and Pak Dae-shik spent his remaining years as a small restaurant owner. Last year, for the first time since immigrating in 1915, his grandmother had returned to her home village on the outskirts of Seoul. In three months she returned to her family in Hawaii and never again spoke of "our country."

***

Frank Gomes was not President of the Hawaii State Senate because of his intelligence, or his loyalties to the establishment, or his favors to special interests, although in all three areas he was highly qualified. He owed his position to being the least offensive to the most people, and to a reputation for fairness. For twenty years the state legislature had been his life, and as Byron Park was led into his well-furnished office his eyes were met with an impressive array of plaques, awards, and autographed pictures of the great and the near great.

"Why would it take five days before anyone found the body?"

"Detective, this is August. We are not in session. In the interim, not too many people are around. This place is deserted, most days. It's not unusual for offices to go undisturbed, unopened, for days at a time. Even weeks." Gomes was fudging a little. Generally, trash was picked up daily, but the staff had been hit by a flu bug and help was a little backed up.

"I understand Senator Bridges was holding interim hearings."

"True. As Chairman of the Senate Health Committee he was looking into the pesticide issue. But his hearings were finished. All that remained was for the Committee to file its report, not due for several months."

"So Bridges had no reason to come to work, on a regular basis, I mean."

"Bridges always came to work. Lots of chairs work full time if they have a big committee. But in this case, I believe he was about to leave on a trip to the mainland. That could be why no one reported him missing. It was natural for no one to miss him."

"Do you know the nature of that trip? Was it official?"

"Yes, official Senate business of a sort. He was to attend some convention on chemicals in San Antonio. Said he felt it was absolutely necessary to keep informed on these issues. So I approved the trip. The

Senate President has to approve all official travel, you know." *I can't let him think this was just another junket. There are enough of those given out every year, to Japan, to Washington. Wouldn't it be ironic if the late Senator Bridges were accused of spending the tax payers' money for a junket? Every year Eastland would refuse such trips. What a pain he was.*

"I understand." *Another damn junket,* thought Park. He glanced at the last few questions on his note pad, anxious to conclude this unproductive interview. "How many people had keys to the Senator's office?

"Our policy is to issue several keys to each legislator. Who they give them to is their business. But if they lose one, it's to be reported immediately. Then we change the lock. Security is pretty good in this building – not perfect – but good. I would imagine that checking with Bridges' secretary would get you the answer to that one." *This guy is really getting nosy. I wonder if he's on to something, or just going through the motions.*

"I see. Well, thank you for your time, Senator. I'll be in touch."

"Feel free to call anytime. And next January, stop in on opening day. Heavy *pupus,* food, fun. Bring along a couple of your buddies. There's plenty to go around." Gomes always liked to end uncomfortable interviews with an invitation. It seemed to leave people with a good impression, and slightly tipped the scales in his favor.

"Thank you Senator. I appreciate that very much, "Park lied.

Come January this guy won't know me from Adam.

As he rode down in the elevator, Park glanced at his notebook to review the basic facts of the case. Bridges was found in a partly decomposed state, obviously dead for at least five days. He was not reported missing. His office was in order, except for a case of pineapple wine, with one bottle opened and nearly empty. Coroner confirmed that he died of a blow to the head suffered from a fall. Gomes reports that it was normal for no one to check in every office during the interim. Next on his list of things to do: meeting with Mei-ling Bridges, 4:30.

***

"Please Mr. Park, don't feel badly about coming. I don't mind answering questions, really. Can I offer you some tea before we begin?"

Mei-ling Bridges was a stunning forty-year-old naturalized citizen, born and raised in Hong Kong. She had met Bridges when he was doing graduate work in Asia. Her family was moderately well-off, but she had learned the value of hard work putting in long hours in the family's import-export business during high school and college. She was proud of her education, her fluency in three languages, and her husband's achievements. There was no doubt that their two-year-old son would be a success in whatever field he chose.

"No thank you, Mrs. Bridges. I really appreciate you seeing me under these difficult circumstances." Park felt a bit intimidated by her polish and graciousness. The home was not a mansion, but both obviously loved Asian art, from the green oriental rug to the broad brush Chinese characters on their scrolls.

"You are investigating his accident?"

"Yes. Just routine. We'd like to know whatever you can tell us about his movements before his death. When exactly was the last time you saw him alive?"

"He was going on a mainland trip. State business. Something about a conference in Texas. It was a good time to go because I was planning to visit my family in Hong Kong. They've never seen our son. He was to join us there after the conference. Let me see, it must have been a week ago Sunday. He played with Jeremy, that's our son, for over an hour before he left for the airport." Mei-ling was trying to be as matter of fact as we could to control her emotions.

"Did he mention anything about stopping at the office?"

"No, not that I can recall, Mr. Park. But it would not be unusual for him to do so. He kept most of his papers there. He could have been picking up some materials for his trip."

"Did he do or say anything unusual during that last week?" Park's eyes surveyed the impressive ceiling-high book shelf. *Bridges must have been quite a reader*, he thought. And yet he was never especially bookish or aloof in school. In fact, he seemed to get along with the poorer students best. It was almost as if he intended to keep his intelligence a secret.

Mei-ling watched Byron Park's gaze move around the room and she was proud that her husband had been a man of ideas as well as of action. She waited for his eyes to return to her before she answered.

"His schedule was always busy, always irregular. That last week was no different. I remember that the weekend before his, his accident, we were going to attend the symphony. At the last minute he got a phone call from someone. I ended up calling a girlfriend to use his ticket and keep me company. I've been to many a concert with a last minute replacement for Eastland. My husband lived for his work, Detective Park."

"Was he in good health?"

"Perfect. It makes it all so hard. If he had been ill, perhaps his death would make sense. But now, it's just a senseless accident. No reason." She was obviously losing her battle to control her feelings. She looked down at the green carpet to compose herself, and Park took the hint.

"Thank you for your time, Mrs. Bridges."

"Quite alright, Detective." As she escorted him to the front door she held his arm and look at him pleadingly. "Please, if you should find anything or think of some information you need, feel free to call."

"I will, Mrs. Bridges," nodded Park respectfully. He wondered if she was trying to communicate something, but he decided not to pursue his vague hunch. He left convinced that there was nothing to add to the official version of the death of Eastland Bridges.

CHAPTER THREE

Helen sat in her second floor capitol office and looked at the plain brown envelop. Its contents, a single page letter, was unaccompanied by an explanation. Eastland had sent it over the Friday before his death, and she had only just worked her way through the usual pile of special reports and constituent letters to its place near the bottom of the "in" tray. She wondered if this was just another piece of legislative trivia.

The sound of the outer door opening reminded her that she had asked Senator Randall Ogawa to stop in before the group met to plan strategy. She was pleased to see his face peek around the corner from the reception area.

"Mind if I come in?" without waiting for an answer the 35-year-old third generation Japanese American strolled in, and noticed that Helen had on his favorite dress. He found her mixture of decisive professionalism and spunky femininity alluring.

"Have a seat, I've got something to show you," she said admitting to herself as Randall leaned over to pull up a chair that he had a cute butt.

She pushed the letter toward him and watched as he read the contents. He tried to concentrate on its meaning while aware of her eyes. *One of these days I've got to have a serious talk about "us"* he thought. The letter was a typical claim for damages addressed to a well-known insurance company. The claimant wrote of health problems associated with polluted wellwater in a rural area of Leeward Oahu.

Randall shrugged. "Another reason why we've got to get these interim hearings going again," he said, anxious that this period between legislative sessions not be wasted.

"Eastland sent it over a few days before his accident."

"Maybe you'd better do some checking. It might provide some ammunition." He nudged the letter towards Helen and was amused that his once radical friend had taken to wearing perfume. Helen slipped the letter into her desk drawer.

"How are we going to handle this meeting," she asked, even though they both knew that she already had it all planned out.

"Patrick will want to analyze our situation step by step. He'll want to be sure he can explain himself after we make our move."

"But will he go along?"

"He will go along. And once he gets his arguments clear, He'll be our most effective advocate," Randall stated with confidence. Patrick Lee, Randall knew, was one of those people who say the world as a rational place, and did his best to live up to this distortion. It was his security blanket, but in the context of politics, public justifications for any actions of consequence were essential. Patrick would provide those justifications better than most.

"Now Bobby is a different story."

At the mention of Robert "Bobby" Martin, Helen rolled her eyes. "Do you think we can pin him down?"

"Oh, he'll climb on board, but will he keep his mouth shut at the hearing?" wondered Randall. He was always so busy trying to demonstrate his understanding of all sides that he muddied the waters. Sandra called him 'Merky Martin.'

Helen thought of the time they had asked Martin to lead the discussion against a bill in committee. In twenty minutes, a clear majority to kill the bill had been turned into a confused collection of undecideds. When the bill had won the required votes to survive, Martin was unable to understand what he had done wrong. "I was only exploring all aspects of the issue," he had whined.

"Sandra is solid," Helen offered.

"No problem. And she'll bring three or four other votes with her."

"Has Wayne gotten back from his treatments on the mainland?"

"He called me to say that he was back, and has his doctor's permission to work Again. He'll be here," Helen said warmly, thinking of how she loved the elderly southerner. Wayne Davis had come to Hawaii to retire from a lifetime in South Carolina politics. In ten years, he had become so involved in senior citizen issues that when asked to run for the Senate he couldn't refuse. He loved public service and the public seemed to love him. Unlike many mainland "haoles", the Hawaiian term for both Caucasian and outsider, he had no trouble gaining acceptance among locals. His sincerity and integrity were unchallenged, and for this he was considered a threat by some circles of the political establishment

They heard the door open and Senator Sandra Shamoto-Burns appeared, full of energy as usual. At 37, she was only four years older than Helen, but her extra weight and conservative fashions made he look well over 50. She was known for her enthusiasm and hard work. In her second four-year Senate term, she was no political lightweight. It helped that she represented the Oahu section of Aiea, considered a very safe district. Something about her ability to mix practical political considerations with idealism had developed a small following in the Senate. The key to her success as Chair of the Conservation Committee was that she could count on at least five solid votes to support her on any issue. In the small 25-member Senate, a group of five could get its way if it played its cards wisely. Helen felt it was a real plus when Sandra had agreed to join Helen's small caucus of younger members. It helped to legitimize their standing with the rest of the Senate.

"Hope I'm not interrupting anything," she winked at Helen. Randall pretended not to notice. "I just saw Bobby in the hall. Looked awfully nervous. Said he'd be over in a minute."

"I appreciate you coming," Helen began. "I know you've been busy with your community association. How is that coming?"

"They are really upset about the Health and Safety Department's recent announcement about the chemical found in our beef," said Sandra. "Last night, we had a pretty lively meeting with over 200 people. The Neighborhood Board sponsored it, and ended up passing a resolution calling for a full investigation. They feel it's the same problem we had several years ago when the pesticides used on lands got into the feed for the cattle, except that time it contaminated the milk. Now it's in the meat itself. They wonder how long this has been going on. To make matters worse, we just found out that the sister of the Board chair has cancer. Nobody knows if it's related, but it sure makes people think about it."

"What's their next step?" Randall asked, thinking that it would be hard to make the connection between the beef issue and the obscure but intriguing letter sent to Helen about water.

"They are apparently willing to go all the way. A subcommittee is looking into the possibility of hiring an attorney. In the meantime, all the members of the board have agreed to either write or call their legislators. Also the Chair was supposed to call the Senate President this morning and demand that the hearings be reopened to deal with the meat issue."

"How will Frank Gomes react to that kind of pressure? "Helen wondered aloud.

"Frank," Sandra noted with a touch of cynicism in her voice, "is a master at avoiding doing what he doesn't want to do. The last thing he wants is to remind people of Eastland Bridges. And since Eastland was chair of the committee, to reopen the hearings is to remind them."

"What about the argument that Eastland had limited his topic to water pollution?" countered Randall. "This is a whole new topic, brought to light by new information."

"That's what the community is counting on. It would be just like a whole new topic, or a whole new hearing. Remember, Eastland is no longer the head of the committee. In cases like this, the Vice Chair takes over," Sandra reminded them.

A look of distress came over both Helen and Randall, for they knew that Richard Tanaka was not likely to see their side of the question. As Vice Chair of the Health Committee he had been at constant odds with Bridges from the start. He even tried to scuttle the idea of holding interim hearings. Losing that fight, he was a tenacious defender of special interests, be they the administration or the chemical and Agricultural industries. During regular legislative sessions his familiar three-piece suit could be spotted leaning over the railing in the open central court of the Capitol, flanked on either side by a well-paid lobbyist, and always surrounded by a cloud of his cigar smoke. When Helen had entered the Senate it was obvious to both of them that they were political enemies. Neither had bothered to waste time getting to know the other.

They were on opposite sides of nearly every important issue, and took each other's opposition for granted. It was only when forced to deal face to face on the Health Committee that they began to see the human side of each other. To Helen, Tanaka was an old-time hack who was probably bought and paid for by corrupt businessmen hoping to hide their crimes. She had been surprised to discover that Richard had a PhD. in agricultural economics and was a big booster of the local 4H clubs. To Tanaka, Helen was a leftist radical who got her kicks from proving that everyone else was less politically virtuous. He was surprised to discover that Helen regularly volunteered her time to work as a nurses' aid in a clinic run by the Catholic Church.

My God, a closet missionary, he said one day to himself, shaking his head. It was an affiliation she had kept to herself, for she unjustly suspected that her liberal friends would find it hard to trust a religiously motivated colleague. In fact, Tanaka was one of the few people who knew. He amusedly held it over her like a mild form of blackmail, occasionally asking her in hushed tones whether the Vatican and the Kremlin could be in agreement. What bothered Helen was that Richard could be almost charming, in his own unsavory way. She sometimes had to remind herself of the damage he inflicted on the environment and the community.

Bobby Martin and Wayne Davis arrived together, discussing something about insurance rates and the lobbyists for that industry. They entered Helen's office, greeted Sandra and Randall, and settled themselves in the worn, green fabric covered swivel chairs with a minimum of small talk about Wayne's health and the prospects of the University of Hawaii football team this fall – Hawaii's tried and true subject of small talk. After everyone had gotten their cups of coffee or cans of pineapple juice, Helen began.

"I guess the purpose of this is to talk about the final report for Eastland's interim hearings. He was about to write it up, and it probably would have been sensational and damaging to the industry. But now Richard is in charge, and I'm afraid by the time session begins next January the only thing we'll have to show for our efforts is a pretty shallow, wishy-washy thing that concludes we have come to no conclusion. What is your feeling about it? Should we just try to get Richard to produce something good, or should we take stronger action?"

Randall was anxious to set the right tone. "I think the first thing we need to recognize is that Richard is just going to bury all the important information from the hearings. If he writes the report, it will be worthless."

"But don't you think that Richard…."

"Let me finish first, Bobby. The second thing is that there are two new pieces of evidence not dealt with in the initial hearings: a complaint about a poisoned well, which Helen just discovered, and this meat thing. We have enough, if we work it right, to force another set of hearings."

"We've got to," Sandra insisted. "Not only do we have more information; I think we have to be honest with ourselves. The first hearings didn't really turn up much concrete evidence. Oh sure, there were a lot of wringing of hands and moaning by some University people. And that new organization, Protect Oahu's Water Resources, what do they call it, POWR, they came out and got some press. And that mainland expert caused a stir. But what have we got? Maybe enough to push for a study. But you know how studies are – depends on who does them. No, we really didn't achieve much in the first set. Eastland could have milked, excuse the pun, as much out of each crumb as possible, but in the end, it was all circumstantial and highly speculative."

"Ah believe Miss Sandra has a point," began Wayne. Ah rememba watchin them chemical dudes. Not a sound out of em. They just sat there like fat frogs on a log after a feast o' flies. Now I ask you to ponder this. If a wildcat is cornered, he fights. But if his escape is open, he lays off in the rocks just outta reach, keeping one ol eye haf open just to make sure. Those fat cats were the same during the hearings. Not a one testified. How come they didn't testify? I'll tell you why. Cuz they weren't threatened, that's why."

Just then Patrick Lee arrived, apologizing for being late. He had heard what Wayne said, and took the interruption caused by his entry to offer a few comments of his own.

"I agree with Wayne. In fact, I heard Richard Tanaka and Ramsey Bingham laughing over Eastland's attempt to "get blood out of a brick," as they put it."

"Ramsey Bingham has always been an arrogant SOB," snapped Helen. "His large hands and bushy eyebrows have gotten the Sandwich Island Chemical Corporation invested into so many other firms that half the town is indebted to him. He must feel completely protected. He never bothers to testify if he doesn't have to. But if it gets a little too close for comfort, you can tell, he shows up just a little less formal than usual, with slightly wrinkled trousers, trying to subtly communicate his indifference. But he shows up just to make sure." Helen had recently gotten into the habit of adding that specific detail about people, their clothes, and their mannerisms. Randall greatly admired Helen for her powers of observation, but at times it seemed to clutter up her speech. She had been reading too many novels he thought, but it added to her attractiveness.

"Patrick, we've just begun talking about what to do about the report," Randall summarized. "There is a general feeling that we really need to reopen the hearings." She looked around the room for nods of agreement.

"Maybe we're being a little hasty," Bobby began. "I mean, what if we really don't uncover anything different. Wouldn't that make us look bad? Maybe we should do a little more digging before pushing for a hearing that might turn out to backfire." Martin was beginning to feel his sweaty palms, which became more uncomfortable as Helen and Randall gave him dirty looks.

"I think you're being too cautious," said Patrick, coming to Bobby's defense by taking his point seriously. It didn't matter to Bobby if people disagreed with him, as long as they took him seriously and showed him a little respect. "It's true we can't predict the outcome of the hearings, but we do have some hard evidence to pursue."

"How would you pursue it," Sandra questioned, delighted to have an opportunity to observe Patrick's considerable powers of analysis. *He was a real asset to the Senate,* she thought, *if only we knew how to use him best. Patrick was a finely crafted tool, an instrument to be applied carefully and skillfully. By himself, caught in the emotions and pressures of legislative logrolling, he would be eaten up. But protected from the harsher aspects of the job, surrounded by an appreciative and committed group, Patrick was a jewel to be polished and displayed.*

"First," Patrick always numbered his sentences if he could, "the Health & Safety Department's new report on stuff in the meat. A whole series of questions. When was this discovered? By whom? If only just discovered, why wasn't the meat tested before? What are the policies for testing? Who decided not to test? If, on the other hand, it had been known for some time, another set of questions? Who decided not to inform the public? What are the standards used to determine if the public has a right to know? Who was informed of the results? Was there a cover-up?

"Second, what is the relationship of state standards, if they exist, to federal standards? What do the mainland people say? Are there other instances of this substance, what is it, TCP or EDB or something, being regulated somewhere else? If so, perhaps we need to bring in someone from another state with the same problem."

Helen loved the fact that she belonged to a small group that could sit through one of Patrick's presentations. Not that many legislators had the patience or the attention span.

"Third, what studies have been done on this substance? You know how long and technical this phase of an investigation can get?"

"Fourth, what is the effect of this substance on children? How many hamburgers do you have to eat before it begins to accumulate in the tissues? Have we done any tests on kids in Hawaii? Maybe we should bring in an expert to outline how such tests would be done and estimate how much it would cost."

Randall glanced at Helen, communicating with his eyes a skepticism that these detailed questions would ever be asked, let alone answered in a public forum.

"Fifth, and perhaps even more important, how did this stuff get into the meat in the first place. It's heptachlor all over again. Somebody sprays the pineapple, the leaves are chopped up and fed to the cattle. The cattle are butchered and eaten by us. The whole agricultural industry could be brought in."

"Sixth, the economic impacts of regulation. You can be sure that Tanaka and his friends are going to bring up this point if we stir up the pot enough. They are going to bring in their economists and tell us how the whole economy will go down the tubes if we prohibit the use of this or that toxic substance. It will be a regular dog and pony show. But that will also give us a chance to probe into their finances. Probe into their use of chemicals. How much? How well regulated? How well protected are the workers? Have any been sick" Any workers' compensation paid to them in chemically related accidents? Where do they store the stuff? Is it transported? There is a lot we can get into if they want to push the economic point."

Thank you Patrick, I think we can get some of this through their computer," said Randall, really trying to turn off Patrick before he turned off the group. They might be more content-oriented than most, but they had their limits too, he thought. "I know someone who has access to the pesticide registration and control files at the Department." Randall did not notice Helen's glow of pride in him, for she genuinely admired Randall's mastery of the mystery of computers. She also enjoyed remembering how much fun they had had that long night he had tried to teach her the 'principles of hacking,' as he put it.

"I'll bet you can Randall," cheered on Sandra, recalling how Helen had spent an entire lunch hour telling her about "Randy" and his talent. She could tell there was more between them than modems and floppy discs.

"We do have the resources," joined Patrick. "We have the contacts. Helen, I'm sure you can get access to Eastland's files, right? Helen nodded, somewhat embarrassed and proud at the same time to acknowledge her 'in' with the Eastland staff.

"And you Bobby," said Randall with an intense stare. Martin almost jumped at the sound of his name. "Didn't you tell me you have been working for Paradise Underwriters? They do business with some of the plantations, right?" Martin swallowed hard and nodded weakly. "You might be able to come up with some dirt on Bingham and his cronies."

"My husband's brother is a land appraiser," offered Sandra, getting into the rhythm of what seemed to Patrick to be more of a pep rally than a strategy session, "and he might be able to help us out in getting some land and tax records. This could be almost enjoyable." Randall agreed to himself it could be fun, using the accumulated experience of several years at the computer terminal, there was no telling just whose code you could break. He was warmed by the pleasant thought of him and Helen working as a team: he with his chosen hobby, and she with an almost uncanny ability to absorb and remember detail. In another world they would be detectives, not politicians.

"Now kids, let's not cheer for the teechdown before the star has caught the pass," Wayne cautioned with his offbeat southern accent. Randall and Sandra had once been driven to hysterics one afternoon as Helen had mimicked Wayne perfectly. Helen had a knack for voices, and was certain that Wayne's accent was somehow a put on. "You still gotta get the votes to reopen the hearins. How you gonna do that? If you kin do that, then we talk about dishin the dirt."

Helen had anticipated Wayne's question and had a plan. "A majority of the committee can force the issue. We need two more votes, as well as the grudging approval of Frank Gomes. Sandra, can you make sure your community people have called Frank?" She nodded and jotted something on a small pad. "Wayne, are you feeling up to a fatherly talk with Richard. Put it to him nicely but strongly that he has no choice. In the meantime, if Randall can talk to Kenji, I'll talk to David."

"How can I be of help?" offered Bobby Martin.

Helen took a deep breath and tried to hide her distress at the man's seeming lack of courage. She decided to let him off the hook, as well as ensuring that he would not foul up the works. "We know you're pretty busy with your work these days, Bobby. Let us handle this end, and we'll let you know as soon as something is decided, OK?" Martin was obviously relieved, but still looked terribly uncomfortable.

The group filed out of Helen's office and promised to meet Again in three days to review their progress. After they had left Helen returned to her desk and began doodling on a yellow legal pad as she mentally reviewed the meeting, measuring each participant's strengths and staying power. Helen was never more serious than when evaluating people, it was what she really loved about politics. In the end, everything came down to motives, character, courage, and values. And topping it off, relationships. "To be really effective," she had once confided to Randy, "we've got to be part detective, part historian, and part psychologist." "You don't think I do this for the money?" he had joked.

Now alone, Helen felt a genuine sense of obligation. She knew it would sound corny to tell anyone, but there was nothing that came closest to choking her up than her sense of duty to Hawaii. It was this love of applying all her faculties to a problem that kept her in politics.

She opened the center drawer and withdrew the envelop with the letter from Eastland. Pulling it out she glanced at the page to confirm her suspicions. It read: "To Paradise Underwriters…." She gazed at the chair where Bobby Martin had been sitting… where he had been uncommonly nervous, and where he had tried to avoid anything which might compromise his job. Looking up a number in her personal telephone directory, she dialed and waited for an answer.

A secretary answered. "Steven Sinclair & Associates, Private Investigators. May I help you?"

CHAPTER FOUR

William Wilcox sat in his tiny, cluttered plantation office. A single 60-watt bulb hung down from the ceiling, casting a dim yellow glow which made everything seem even older and dirtier. He poured yet another glass of Suntory Whiskey, the last of his birthday bottle. It was more than just another shallow gift from a legislative staff member to a lobbyist. This was special. This was from Betsy Ito, a lady Wilcox was growing terribly fond of.

Wilcox was a lonely man. Since his wife had left him for neglect years ago, he had devoted his large, rugged body to the demands of running a modern sugar business. For a long time, this was a satisfying obsession, but in the last few years he was growing weary of the dusty red earth and the mounting paperwork. His occasional duties as lobbyist for the sugar industry were welcome relief from the daily pressures of agriculture, and there were other amenities. He had found himself enjoying the easy banter with the capitol staff. Unlike the noisy and dirty plantation, the capitol was clean, quiet, and filled with well dressed women.

It was odd, he thought, that the secretary of the man most feared by his industry he would find the most attractive. Betsy Ito, loyal member of Eastland Bridges' legislative team for years, never let professional differences or politics diminish her flashing eyes, her charm, and her aloha for all who entered their office.

In spite of the rough exterior of Bill Wilcox, Betsy had seen something gentle and decent in this man just two years her senior. They both came to look forward to his visits. He remembered one evening towards the end of the last session when staff and lobbyists lingered in the halls waiting for word form the marathon conference committees. Wilcox had sat and talked with Betsy for three hours; flirted really. He had teased her about her eyes, and she had blushed like a school girl. They were both in their late forties, and more vulnerable than they would admit. Later he had sent her flowers, "To B. from B.," and she had given him a bottle of his favorite whiskey for his birthday. He asked her out to dinner on the last day of session, and she promised to accept when she got back from visiting her relatives in L.A. It wasn't until three weeks ago that he saw her again.

Wilcox stared at the two letters he had just composed in longhand. One, a report to a distant boss he seldom saw. It was brief and contained only the minimum amount of information required to assure the recipient that all his tracks were covered. As he reread its contents, he regretted that he was called upon to use people he cared for. He had deliberately distorted a relationship to give the impression that his friendship with Betsy was merely an extension of a larger plan to manipulate.

The second letter was even more troublesome. Blackmail was not what he had expected. *Why did they have to pick me to do the dirty work?* He thought. He knew the answer. *They chose someone just smart enough to carry out the orders, but not shrewd enough to make trouble. Someone whose career would benefit by the success of the crime. And he had benefitted, hadn't he? A new house, two new cars, plenty of 'business trips' to Vegas and New York.* All of that he had accepted because the larger purpose was the health of the industry. He could find idealism in that. But this blackmail thing, this was different.

A third letter he now began, and in it he unconsciously attempted to balance out the unseemly in his life with the wholesomeness he yearned for. He had never expressed his true feeling to Betsy, but now all his emotions, his loneliness, and his affection took hold of his hand. He was candid. He was gentle. He tried not to sound too pushy, but he was perfectly open. "*Please be part of my life,*" he pleaded. "*I need you, and we can share our joys of our remaining years together,*" he continued. The whiskey prevented him from recognizing the melodrama in his words, but even if he had he probably would have left it in anyway. He letter was a purging, and effort to deny with love for his Betsy the awful things represented in the other two letters.

When he was done he carefully folded each into an identical white envelope. As he picked up his pen to address them his privacy was interrupted by the glare of the headlights through the window and the squeal of tires. He hastily shoved the three envelopes into the desk and rose to meet his visitor.

Ramsey Bingham, wearing high boots and riding britches, stalked into the small office and let Wilcox know by his expression that he was not happy.

"What, drunk again?"

"I'm alright. What do you want?" Wilcox sat down again and held his glass.

"We've got to get those documents into the right filing cabinets. And we've got to do it before those damn politicians start snooping around. Have you arranged for another meeting to transfer the letters?"

"Just about to send it out in the mail. What are you worried about? He's in our pocket already. He so scared that his family and friends are going to find out he'll do anything. Just leave it to me," concluded Wilcox, trying to sound as confident and in charge as Bingham. He looked at his well-dressed collaborator and decided that he couldn't stand his upper class pretentions. Bingham was a grad of Punahou High School, THE elite private school in Hawaii, and from there it was Harvard Business School, then home to join the family business. Now he was president of the Sandwich Island Chemical Company and sat on the boards of directors of a half a dozen others. *What is a man like this doing with blackmail?* Wilcox asked himself.

"Just leave it to you? Look what happened the last time we just left it to you. You're a bungler, Wilcox. A good business manager, when you're sober, but in the end a bungler. See that you do it right this time, and no slip ups."

Wilcox sipped his whiskey as he listed to Bingham's car disappear down the narrow road. *Someday I'm going to punch that sonnovabitch in the nose and leave all this,* he thought. Still thinking of Betsy, he pulled the three envelopes form the drawer, hastily addressed and stamped them, and slipped them into his attaché case for mailing the next day. He pulled the string on the light bulb and lurched out to his jeep. In ten minutes he pulled up to his new and empty house, to spend another sleepless night.

***

The next morning, as Bill Wilcox was still trying to recover from his whiskey and his guilt, and the Sunday sun welcomed another beautiful day in the Islands, Steven Sinclair slipped the special key he had been given and activated the door to the private Senate elevator. *Sunday morning was perfect*, he thought. *No one around. No need to alert the authorities by using a flashlight at night.* He cautiously peered out the elevator door on the second floor and quickly moved down the hall to his destination.

The office key worked perfectly and he silently opened and closed the door which read: SENATOR EASTLAND BRIDGES, CHAIR, and SENATE COMMITTEE ON HEALTH. The office was apparently untouched from the day they had found the body. He immediately noticed the case of pineapple wine at the far end. One bottle was missing. He looked behind a desk and saw an empty bottle and a plastic glass at the bottom of a waste basket. He made a mental note, and moved toward Bridges' private office.

Steven Sinclair has been a private investigator for ten years, and was regarded as a kind of exotic celebrity by the younger professionals in Honolulu. At the price of answering stupid questions at cocktail parties, Sinclair was able to make contacts and gain access and information that other, less connected investigators were unable to match. It was one of these cocktail party acquaintances that had led to a genuine appreciation and friendship with several legislators, including his client on this case, Helen Tokugawa.

It was clear form the newspaper reports that officials had no suspicions of foul play in the death of Eastland Bridges. Regardless of Helen's loyalty, Sinclair could not help but think they were probably right. But you never knew. The insurance letter could be nothing, or it could lead to a more interesting explanation of events.

Bridges' private office was exactly as Ethyl had described it. Sinclair had been impressed at the custodian's powers of visual recall. "I can tell you where very one keeps his waste basket and what's usually in it," she had joked. She was surprised to be considered important enough for someone like a private detective to be interested.

"I don't know what you want to know that I haven't already told that nice detective with the mustache. He was a Korean, you know. Don't believe we've ever had a Korean legislator," she remarked as her eyes evaluated the serious but friendly man in his mid-thirties.

Ethyl's small walk-up apartment in the Kapahulu district was modest and a bit cluttered with movie magazines. Her black and white cat snoozed at the foot of her peach-colored sofa. She did not like to be reminded of the unpleasant circumstance which had precipitated her retirement. But after a week at home she was glad to have someone to talk to.

"I must have gone through that day ten times with the detective. I'm sure you've read the reports, if you're as good an investigator as Magnum," she teased.

"So you approached the door of Bridges' office. Was there anything at all that was a clue to what you would find?"

"Nothing, except if you mean the smell. There was a strange odor. Now that I think of it I'll never forget it. But at the same time, it was just another strange smell. I thought someone had left out some food or something."

"You approach the door. Is it locked?"

"No, now that you mention it, it was unlocked. Closed, but unlocked."

"You open the door. What is the first thing you see?"

"I guess the first think I can remember was that awful odor was really, really strong. Nothing was different in the office. Just like I told the detective. All normal.

"So you immediately walked toward the inner office and…"

"I immediately, yes that's right. I went right to the office…and you know the rest. Horrible. I hope I never have to find, you know, somebody in that state again.

"Did you walk quickly? Did you stop to do anything on the way? Straighten anything out? Pick anything up?"

"Oh yeah, I picked up a small piece of paper. I remember because I pulled the cart into the path anyone would take to walk in and out. That's why I ran into it on my way out."

"Can you remember anything about the paper?"

"It was a memo, or scrap of something. Yes, I think it was from Bridges' memo pad. No wait. It was from somewhere else and had a room number on it. I guess it was the number of Bridge's office. As for the memo paper itself, I do remember it because it was bordered with blue palaka. You know what palaka is? It's that kind of checkerboard weave they make local shirts out of. Looks a little like the old Italian table cloths, except the lines are thicker. Well it had that boarder and I think it said something like Palaka Co. Or Palaka Corporation or something."

Remembering a prominent ware house firm, Sinclair offered, "Palaka Produce?"

"That's it. Palaka Produce. Well maybe. Could be it. Hard to remember exactly with so many other things happening that day you know."

"So you now enter the office. I know this is unpleasant, but please try to bear with me. Apart from the body, is there anything you noticed?"

"Yes. As I told the police, the waste basket was knocked over. I guess it happened when he, Senator Bridges, God rest his soul, when he fell, huh?"

It has been just a hunch for Sinclair to visit Ethyl, but now he was glad he took the time.

Moving quickly Sinclair identified a coffee mug on the desk which read "Da Senatah" as one which must have belonged to Bridges. He removed a small box from his innocuous looking back pack, and spread out the fingerprint kit on the desk. First, he carefully applied the powder and dusted the mug. He eyes next were drawn to the filing cabinet just in back of the desk. The top drawer was slightly opened. He repeated the same procedure for prints on the handle. Finally, he returned to the outer lobby and carefully, using his handkerchief, retrieved the bottle and the plastic glass from the waste basket. Removing the evidence from these items, he carefully returned everything to its original place, taking care to remove any prints he might have left.

He left the office and descended the stairs to avoid running into any particularly conscientious legislators in the elevator, or worse yet, a security guard.

As Sinclair rode his ten speed away from the capitol building his mind began to examine every piece of evidence he had assembled, and his imagination went wild with the possibilities he might find when he analyzed the fingerprints. *It was strange*, he thought, *that the police were so quick to believe the obvious, that Bridges was merely a drunken politician who fell down and killed himself on his desk. What a cynical view they must have of life*, he thought. *Not even the benefit of the doubt. Not even the decency to look further than their noses.*

The early morning brightness was now filtered through a bank of clouds moving off of the steep mountains and out of the valley. He could see a rainbow straight ahead on Nuuanu Avenue as he pedaled up a slight incline. Another great day to watch the football games and then hit the beach.

CHAPTER FIVE

Barbara Lum carried the extension cords for her camera man past the railing to the capitol's inner courtyard on the second floor, and into the Senate Committee's hearing room. She was careful not to let the dirty wires soil her expensive midi-dress, a copy of a Paris original. In her high heels and makeup, she was a bit overdressed for the hearing, as many TV women tended to be. She was a 32-year-old professional on the rise, and already a familiar face to thousands of Hawaii residents. She had even managed to break through the stereotype *'local news and color'* reports, often reserved for the pretty face and the lilting voice, to hard news, and occasionally substitute anchor spots on the nightly news.

It was a slow news day, as Monday's always were, and there didn't seem to be much more happening than this curious and hastily called interim hearing on chemicals found in local meat. There was no doubt that the issue was of interest to the public, but there was just so much you could do with a formal hearing. Lots of talking heads, she thought, privately referring to the media term for a person talking to the camera with no other action going on.

Several weeks ago, before the death of the Chairman, she had gone through a whole routine: the background reports, and the interviews. In her view, the public needed a little rest from this one. Besides, it was during the interim, between sessions, not a time of heightened interest in legislative business. But her boss had insisted, especially after the personal phone call from a confidential political source that a surprise witness might appear. *Politicians were always trying to get mileage over that one*, she felt. *Always trying to use the media for their own political purposes.* Smiling to herself, she acknowledged that the media did as much 'using' as anyone.

The room was empty except for a staff member from the Committee who was laying out folders and ID signs for Senators expected to attend.

She and her camera man quickly spotted the outlets and began to set up their camera and lights, grateful that they had beat the crowd. As he completed the preparations, she went off down the hall to the lady's room to ensure that her hair and makeup were ready to appear on the six o'clock news.

By the time she returned, a number of lobbyists and legislators had already arrived, and she could begin her task of piecing together another quickie sixty second, in depth report on what a terrible thing it was to have chemicals in the meat. That would be her first angle. Fallback would be any squabble that might arise between the politicians. A gift from the gods would be a surprise witness that actually provided some hard news and more than five people were deeply interested in.

Chairman Richard Tanaka strolled into the room and almost sat down when he noticed Barbara Lum heading his way. He attempted to retreat into the inner staff office but she intercepted him with her eyes and he could not escape without looking guilty of something. *They always try to make you look guilty*, he thought.

"Hello Barbara, you're looking nice today."

"Thank you Senator. Can you tell me why the Committee decided to reopen the chemical pollution hearings?" She noticed that he was looking at her hair and was pleased that Mr. Timothy had squeezed her in for an appointment that morning.

"As you know, Barbara, we did receive some new information about a possible problem with our meat. Now we really don't know if there is a contamination situation, but we thought the public had a right to know. So we decided to reopen and see what we could find out. Will you excuse me for a moment?" He deftly left her without the usual follow-up assault as he strode through the off limits door and let it close slowly behind him.

Barbara Lum was no fool. She could tell that Tanaka had been pressured into holding the hearings. It was clear that several members of the committee, Helen Tokugawa, Sandra Shamoto-Burns, to name a few, were mavericks. How they had managed to reopen, or even more importantly, why they had wanted to reopen the hearing, was something she was determined to find out.

It was her habit to list everyone of importance who attended any function she covered. Her narrow reporter's notebook read: Chair – Tanaka; Sens – Tokugawa, Ogawa, Davis, Shamoto-Burns, Lee, Thompson, Matson, Richards, Rodrigues. Reps – Robinson, King, Chang. These last three were invited to participate as they were members of the House Committee on Health, which would handle similar matters in the lower chamber. Also present in the room were an assortment of observers and lobbyists, the most prominent was Ramsey Bingham. He was sitting next to a very tall very fair haired muscular man to whom he never spoke.

It was one of the smaller hearing rooms so that the chairs of the senators at the table were just in front of the observers. Very intimate, and without the sense that the public was separate from the process. She preferred these more "democratic" hearing rooms, as she thought of them, not only because it was easier to hear what was said, but also because it was more inviting for genuine dialogue. Observers, if they had enough stature, and if the hearing was informal enough, might actually engage the legislators in a discussion. In the larger hearing rooms in the House, the members sat at a huge koa wood table separated from the public. Government was least accessible in those settings, she felt.

Often you could see the inexperienced blue collar worker or housewife or teacher sitting there, completely intimidated by the surroundings. *There are the men and women of power and here am I, the lowly peasant pleading me case,* she imagined them to be thinking. Curious how the most everyday things, the size of the room, the placement of chairs and their relative comfort – cushy for the officials, hard for the public – the intensity of the air conditioning, all these had an impact on democracy, she reflected. She caught her mind and emotions wandering, feeling almost angry at how government and business alike designed and arranged things for the powerful, and how so seldom did they think of the sensibilities of the powerless.

The first 'witness" was not a citizen nor a lobbyist, but Senator Shamoto-Burns providing some background on the crisis in Hawaii's meats. Using a chart mounted on an easel next to Tanaka's chair, Shamoto-Burns recited how many tons of beef were grown in Hawaii, the average per-capita consumption, daily consumption, and the differences between children and adults in their nutritional needs.

Her next chart revealed the major ranches in Hawaii, the tons of feed used annually, and the use of chemicals to treat that feed, preventing losses from pests and diseases. Also presented were estimates as to the pesticide and other toxic substances applied to plants used in feed. It was a thorough, informative, and boring barrage which, Barbara noticed, few people could follow closely due to the Senator's excited speech. There were too many facts and figures. Too little time to digest it all. The only clear effect was that Chairman Tanaka was made uncomfortable by having to view the whole thing over his shoulder. In spite of the gulf between the data and the minds of those present, Shamoto-Burns had set the tone for the meeting. It would be one where hard evidence was to be in the forefront of discussion. Or so she expected.

Following her lecture, there was a pause, and it was evident that few in the room wanted to expose their meager knowledge to compare with what had preceded. "Any questions?" asked the Chair. After a suitable interval when no member of the committee spoke, Representative Michael Robinson nodded his head and was recognized.

"How reliable are these figures? I was under the impression that the State did not keep regular records of such things." Helen glanced at Randall and they knew the challenge had been accepted.

"It is true some of these are estimates," Shamoto-Burns began, "but they do provide us with a sense of the size of the problem"

"Who said there was a problem?" the Chair asked a little too anxiously.

"We know as a result of the recent tests that some of these chemicals have been found in the meat. We know that many chemicals are unhealthy for us. We don't know enough about the situation to say there is or there is not a health risk, but I for one am thankful for the Senator bringing these facts to our attention," countered Randall Ogawa.

Jim Thompson, a high school classmate of Chairman Tanaka, sought to slow down what he felt would become an uncontrolled blast of rhetoric. To diffuse this issue, he thought, required a relentless calm, steady hand, a seasoned voice, a reassuring probe. "I agree that the situation requires careful examination," he said slowly, "and that is why the Chairman's question should be considered. I, for one, am not an expert; and so I don't really know what are facts and what are opinions."

Shamoto-Burns, wary of letting the discussion get bogged down in a debate over the validity of her figures, explained, "The data is a combination of information on chemicals, nutrition polling, sales by supermarkets, and tax records. The Department of Health & Safety, who we will hear from later, does attempt to keep an inventory of chemicals used in the State. But I would agree that more work needs to be done on coming up with meaningful and valid figures to assist the committee. In fact, one thing we should look into is why the State does not have a better handle on this data," she finished, glad to have thought of another angle to support the need for legislation.

Barbara Lum was growing a little impatient. She could see the discussion was just part of the preliminary sparing that always went on when two strongly held positions were presented. Obviously there were people in the room who wanted to emphasize the problem, and there were also people who would rather it went away. The only novelty was the open debate between legislators, which seldom went on at a public hearing, but which sometimes surfaced in these less formal meetings during the interim.

The first testifier was John Logan of the Environmental Protection Agency. His dark beard, horn rimmed glasses, and Boston accent set him off as both an outsider and an authority. He was well practiced in testifying at mainland hearings, and his content-laden remarks and institutional jargon were a reminder to all present of the countless subtle and fundamental assumptions that bound together Hawaii's political culture. It was also a reminder of the distance between Washington and Honolulu. That distance made old timers like the Chairman defensive, Barbara reasoned. Defensiveness was expressed as hostility or even ridicule of non-local styles. Still, she felt, this authoritative 40-year-old in a suit and tie would be seen as an expert beyond the reach of conventional put-downs. If he had anything of substance to say, and it was understandable, he could be a difficult one for the Chairman to handle.

"The chemical found in Hawaii's meat has been identified as Triptathal, or TTT, a known carcinogen," he began, naming for the first time the culprit, and immediately giving credence to 'the problem.' "We know, according to tests done at Stanford University last year, that TTT can accumulate in muscle tissue of rats, and that over time it can be associated with a number of cancers," which he, to Tanaka's chagrin, proceeded to enumerate. "In addition, we know that such accumulations are likely to more directly affect infants and children under the age of ten more than adults by a factor of five. "

Melvin Richards, the oldest man in the Senate at the Age of 81, was as sharp as he was when he was Speaker of the House, and later President of the Senate. He could recognize that this mainlander was going to cause more trouble than anticipated. *Why did Richard even let this guy in the room?* He wondered.

"Mr. Morgan," he interrupted, intentionally using the wrong name, "how many of your rats regularly eat Hawaiian hamburgers?" The question cut the atmosphere of formality, and as the chuckles died down John Logan gave Richards a look which betrayed his true contempt for the smallness of Island politicians. It was a mistake, for as every legislator knew, allowing the opposition to know your weaknesses was an invitation to disaster. Richard caught the look, and warmed to the attack on his self-wounded prey.

"What I mean to say, Mr. Morgan…"

"Logan, Senator, the name is Logan."

"What I mean to say, Mr. Lohhhgan, is that we have heard this kind of thing before. Your rats keep dying, and we keep living. How do you account for this, young man?"

"In most cases, when rodents have problems, later on we discover humans have problems too," he explained, losing the confidence in his voice. "But it is not something that usually expresses itself right away. Many cancers take ten or twenty years or more before being detectable."

"So what you're telling us is that it will be twenty years before you are sure of anything, right?"

"Well, in some cases it might be that long. But in many.…"

"Thank you son, you answered my question. Mr. Chairman, sir, I don't believe this fellow can help me very much. Ye see, I doubt if

I'll be around to find out if his rats were right." Another round of muffled guffaws from like-minded supporters of the Chairman served to emphasize Richards' point.

Helen had had reservations about the EPA testimony right from the start. In the first place, the EPA need only issue a statement. No need to put someone on the stand, as it were, as a target. Now the hard evidence presented had been compromised by a homey dismissal. Richards was still respected and loved by of the Senate, in spite of what even the aging Wayne Davis felt was laziness, to make a direct challenge unwise. Maybe the press will pick up the right stuff, Helen hoped, as she glanced at Barbara Lum across the room. Helen was startled to find that Lum was not watching Logan or Richards, but her! As if she recognized Helen's judgment on Logan. Helen began to feel uncomfortable, and quickly shifted her eyes back to Logan, and then down to some papers in front of her.

The rest of Logan's testimony passed with a few inquiries on both sides, but no important revelations. Nearly everyone was glad when it was over. Logan left the room unable to tell whether or not anyone was really interested in what he had to say. Barbara Lum resisted her desire to interview the 'smart hunk' as she stereotyped him, and focused her attention on the next witness, Clarence Soong, manager of the Leeward Pineapple Plantation.

Soong's testimony was predictable, but sincere. A true believer in plantation agriculture, Soong wanted all to know how economically important the industry was. He wanted people to appreciate the jobs, the revenues, and the open space. All that was good, in his view.

Randall Ogawa found it most difficult to deal with the Clarence Soongs of Hawaii. In many ways, there were right. Sugar and pine kept Hawaii green. Agriculture, he had always believed, was better than heavy industry with belching smokestacks. In years past Ogawa had marched on the Department of Agriculture demanding the protection of Hawaii's agricultural lands, which in effect meant protection for sugar and pine. Environmentalists like Ogawa had been forced psychologically into the habit of defending sugar and pine in order to prevent the urbanization of agriculture lands. Urbanization, in Ogawa's view, was just another get rich quick scheme of developers who wanted to build luxury single family estates when most island residents needed affordable housing.

Ogawa could remember those intoxicating meetings when the unions and the sugar managers had met with the environmentalists to plan a common strategy against a development on Kauai. *Those were the days*, Ogawa thought. *We actually felt there was the possibility of a lasting coalition.* But then the recession had killed the development, and the need for continued cooperation evaporated.

Helen knew that Randall and Clarence had a good relationship and respected their friendship. But she could not separate the production of pineapples and sugar from the application of toxic chemicals. It was common knowledge that the plantations sold their left-over wastes to feed lots for cattle. If those wastes were laced with chemicals, that's what the cattle ate. She could see Randall's respect for Soong, or perhaps it was the nostalgia for the days of protest and mobilization. She also noticed Randall began to play with his pencil in a certain way, which he always did when he was uncertain. She knew he would not be able to objectively dismantle Soong's assumptions.

"Mr. Soong," she said calmly and respectfully, "the Pineapple Planters Association has been around for how long?"

"Over eighty years, Senator. They were organized after the turn of the century for the purpose of carrying on research as well as promoting agriculture in the Islands," he answered with pride.

"Isn't it true that initially the industry relied primarily on biological pest controls?"

"That's right. We imported quite a few species for pest control, just like the sugar companies. One major one, a real success, was the insect eating toad."

"But now you use mainly pesticides, is that right?" Helen continued.

"That's right, they are much cheaper, and much easier to control. You know what happened with the mongoose," Soong laughed. The mongoose was imported to control rats, but the mongoose slept while the rats ate, and vice versa, so now the Islands were overrun with mongoose for no purpose.

"Have you done any research lately on biological pest controls?"

"Not really. The main problems of late have been the price of pine on the mainland and getting into the fresh fruit markets. Our efforts have shifted to product promotion. We still do some research, but for the most part, our resources, as an association that is, are involved with marketing."

"Among the chemicals you use is TTT?"

Soong, ever attentive to small details, referred to his annual report which listed the chemicals presently under use. "Well, as a matter of fact, we discontinued use of TTT a few years ago. We have more effective compounds today."

Helen was appalled at the thought of what those 'more effective compounds' might be, but she chose to pursue the previous point. "Why did you discontinue its use?" she asked innocently, knowing the reason and wanting the press to hear it.

"The EPA banned it in Hawaii, Senator," answered Soong somewhat meekly.

"And it was already banned on the mainland, correct, Mr. Soong?"

"That is correct."

"Doesn't that bother you, Mr. Soong, to be using chemicals already banned on the mainland, just because you could get an exception out of the EPA?"

Soong was growing uneasy. Ramsey had promised him that there would be no trouble. "Just give us a little pep rally for agriculture." He had advised. But some of these people were beginning to sound hostile.

"Senator," the Chairman broke in, "you make it sound as if Mr. Soong were on trial. He's just here to give us his perspective on the importance of the pineapple industry. Thank you Mr. Soong, we appreciate your time."

Barbara Lum was surprised that Senator Tokugawa would allow the Chairman to cut her off like a school girl talking out of turn. *These politicians*, she thought, *were so complex. Always involved in little soap operas, and impossible to predict.* Yet her observations were not without admiration. *They were often willing to take a lot of baloney to promote their bills and their causes,* she felt. Lum made a note of Soong's remarks on the use of TTT, and on it having been banned on the mainland but used in Hawaii. This might even be worth a lead for the evening news she thought, and directed the camera man to pan across the room and make sure he focused on Soong for a few seconds, just long enough to slap some graphics under his head later on.

Lum also noticed that Soong was being treated with deference. He was not the sort of person who would use or abuse power, she guessed, checking out his modest attire. No, it was not out of fear they let him off, it was out of respect. He was obviously doing the best job he could, in all sincerity. For all the questionable behavior of politicians, Barbara had to admit to herself they seldom publically embarrassed people who were not tough enough to take it.

Soong nodded gratefully to the Chairman, shuffled his papers, and receded to the back row next to Ramsey Bingham, who patted him on the back reassuringly. Ramsey was a large man, similar to Lyndon Johnson, Lum recalled. Johnson was known for his imposing physical presence, and his large hands. Bingham had those hands. And when he put one on your shoulder, it was hard to refuse his request. He made you want to work for him. People lived for the chance to be appreciated by such men.

As Ramsey Bingham laid his appreciative hand on Clarence, and as Michael Robinson rose to mix himself some instant coffee on the staff table behind the Chairman, Thelma Winters, of the Leeward Community Action Coalition, took her seat. She was a middle aged woman who enjoyed playing her ukulele at parties, and was full of a certain county swagger. Her large forearms spoke of a life of physical work, and she was clearly not someone to take lightly. As a part-Hawaiian, she felt she had as much right to be there as anyone.

"Mr. Chairman, mahalo for allowing me to give my *mana'o* - that's opinion for your *haole* boys," she winked, "to your committee. I am just a simple woman, a simple Hawaiian. I cannot understand all your fancy numbers, Mr. Chairman. All I know is that my grandchildren love to eat meat and drink water. And now this man from the EPA has come and tells us that maybe the water and meat are not so good for us. Maybe they cause cancer or something. This I do not understand, Mr. Chairman. I have always taught my *keikis*, my children, to respect the government. The government is your friend, I always say. The government will protect you. But now, what am I to say when they ask why they cannot eat or drink?"

Barbara Lum gave her camera man an elbow in the side that nearly knocked him off his chair. He quickly rose and began filming what would probably be the most eloquent person at the hearing.

"Mr. Chairman, members of this Committee," she continued, using a tired and pleading voice that spoke of both gentleness and dignity, "what am I to tell the *keikis* of our community when they ask, 'Auntie, why can't we eat the meat?' I come before you today as a mother, as a grandmother, and as Chair of the Leeward Community Action Coalition. The Coalition wishes to first object to these hearings being held during the day. Mr. Chairman, our people are hardworking people. Some of us work in Mr. Soong's plantation. Some work in small businesses. Some are housewives tending their small children. We cannot be running down here to your fancy buildings every day. You should come out to us. So the first demand of our Coalition, Mr. Chairman, is that you bring your staff and your media friends out to the country where our people are, at night when they don't have to work."

"The second demand of our Coalition, is that all use of these chemicals be stopped immediately. We don't know if they are causing illness. And we don't know if, what did the mainland man say, twenty years? We don't know what will happen to us in twenty years. But we are not," her voice rose with power, "not going to be guinea pigs. You have no right to use us as if we were slaves or animals."

Simple person bullshit, thought Thompson. *This lady knows what she is doing. She has every guilty bone in every liberal body wrapped around her little finger. I've heard these Hawaiians give the same sad story speech time and time Again. They try to intimidate you with the Bury-my-heart-at-wounded-knee line.* Thompson was not really as cynical as his thoughts made him feel. He was just resentful that Thelma Winters was on the verge of getting the best of him again.

"The third demand of the Coalition is that the State begin an ongoing monitoring of all Hawaii's foods to determine just what chemicals we are subjecting our *keiki* to. We feel these three demands are reasonable, Mr. Chairman. *Mahalo.*"

Tanaka was certain that something had to be done to turn the tide from what he considered to be an emotional appeal. He was pleased when good old reliable Melvin Richards indicated his desire to speak. Richards was still fairly vigorous for his Age, distaining special treatment for a growing loss of hearing. His full head of hair helped give him extra stature.

"Mrs. Winters," Richards began slowly, "just to clarify things, could you explain just who belongs to this coalition?"

"The Leeward Community Action Coalition, Senator, is made up of community leaders throughout the Leeward Oahu coast. We represent nearly every neighborhood group from Pearl Harbor to Makaha. The Coalition was formed recently because of concern over the pollution of our air, our waters, and our food."

"So you are a fairly new group?"

"Our neighborhood members and leaders have been around for a long time."

"But the coalition, the coalition is new. And how many citizens do you claim to represent?"

"I said, the Leeward…"

"Mrs. Winters, I realize you consider yourself an advocate of Leeward residents, but my question is just how many actually belong to your group? Do you have a membership list we could see?" Richards was using a common tactic to discredit the legitimacy of a citizen-based group. When put in a bind, legislators sometimes resorted to this, and in some cases they were right in asserting that an elected official did indeed represent more people. In this case, however, Thelma knew that Richards was off-base, and she searched her mind for an appropriate response that would not too harshly reflect her anger.

"Senatah Richards," began Wayne Davis, the only other senior citizen on the Committee who could go round for round on the same emotional turf as Richards, "you know full well that community associations are not equipped with secrahtrys to type fancy lists for fancy senatahs. Ah do believe this young lady represents a legitimate outfit, an thet we'd better watch our peas 'n cues ifn we cross 'em."

"I will defer to my MAINLAND colleague on this point, but I would only point out that community outfits are also not equipped with trained chemists who know what they're doing," snapped Richards.

"Mrs. Winters, as Chairman of this Committee, it is, as you know, my responsibility to gather the very best information possible. You have made three demands, although I know you meant to say requests, of this Committee. I wonder, did your coalition do any research as to how much these requests might cost the State of Hawaii?"

"Mr. Chairman, "said Thelma gravely, having shifted into a mode of great solemnity and purposeful humility, 'we are only poor citizens. We don't understand all your technical words and legalese. We only want you to do what is right. Of course we can't tell you how much to the last penny these demands will cost. But neither can you tell us how much ignoring the problem will cost. We only know that the costs of our demands are in dollars, and the costs of no action might be in the lives of our children."

Barbara Lum was pleased that the camera man had recorded this last exchange. It would make the centerpiece of her story. She was filled with admiration for this Hawaiian lady who was able to use her considerable intelligence and culture to make a point with dignity and elegance. No matter what the Chairman and his friends said now, the testimony of Thelma Winters would stand as a highlight, perhaps the only memorable highlight, of this hearing.

Chairman Tanaka, a master of sensing momentum, chose to declare a ten-minute recess. Several senators retreated to the inner office, a few stopped to greet observers on their way to the rest room, and a number of people went outside to smoke cigarettes over the railing of the inner court yard. Barbara Lum wanted to take the opportunity to interview Winters, but the feisty activist hurried off to attend a family gathering in Ala Moana Park.

***

Ryan James was the perfect choice to defend an unpopular policy. At 37, he was the youngest member of the cabinet, head of the beleaguered State Department of Health and Safety. His curly hair, wing tipped shoes, and corduroy jacket made him look like a bright ambitious lawyer trying his first case. Like many competent but inexperienced professionals, James attempted to balance his youth with conservative postures. He sought to prove his maturity by reflecting the values of the establishment. If loyalty to the administration were desired, he would be its most ardent defender. If political debts required an easing of environmental barriers to development, he would find dozens of ways to facilitate that development.

In part, this was made possible by James' past involvement as a lobbyist for carefully chosen environmental causes. His rise to fame from the chairman of a neighborhood board to a prominent delegate to the State's Constitutional Convention protected him from charges of being out of touch with people. There were those, like Randall Ogawa, who felt Ryan James' transformation from advocate of reform to defender of the status quo was made all too smoothly. "Very cool and very slick," Randall told Helen. "It's hard to put your finger on why he is so objectionable. He's always well-prepared, always articulate."

"And always looking out for No. 1," Helen added.

She could not forget a recent luncheon with a girl friend who worked in the Health and Safety Department. "The staff meetings are always the same," Susan complained. "First Ryan spends 20 minutes telling us how hard he's been working. He's full of chatty stories of what he said to the Governor, or what some other department head had confided in him. This is followed by a show and tell session, where very staff member tells what they've been working on. Finally, the man gives out assignments."

"What's wrong with that?" Helen had asked.

"What's wrong is that he's a one-man-show. No one can do it as well as he can, so he thinks. He never once has said, 'I have to make a decision and I'd like your opinion.'" Helen noticed that Susan had lost interest in her salad and was waving her fork in the air.

"Is it possible that you're jealous that he's gotten so far so soon?" Helen chided.

"I've thought about that, and sometimes I do feel jealous. But it's more than that. When you work in the government, everyone, deep down, wants to make a contribution. You want to feel you are part of the team, not a flunky to some star performer, but a co-contributor. Ryan makes us feel more like a bunch of incompetents. 'Staff does not make policy,' he always says. It's a question of respect. There are dozens of experienced and dedicated people in our department. They could and should be part of important decisions. But under Ryan James we are all minor flunkies. A lot of people want more out of their jobs."

"Maybe he's just trying to get your department moving again, you know, instead of the tail wagging the dog," Helen offered. She knew that many department heads were constantly frustrated by the inability to get their department to go along. *The public thinks executives have all this power*, she reflected, *but they can't do as much as people think. The civil servants, the accountants, the program managers, they all have tenure. The department heads don't.*

"You don't get people to join a parade by making them clean up after the horses," Susan blurted out, and then laughed at the unwitting richness of her analogy. "People love to be asked. You ask them, you include them, and they'll do anything for you. There is so little direct praise given out that with a little tact and attention you can have these white collar types eating out of your hand. That's the sad part about it all. It doesn't have to be this way."

"You sound like this is a big problem."

"You don't know how demoralizing it is. There's this guy I know who is a planner. You wouldn't believe how enthusiastic he was, how excited when he was hired. This was his dream, to get a regular job and to use his knowledge. And do you know what he's doing? Not planning. He's compiling statistics to be used in the Governor's speeches. They won't let him even get near an important project. When he's not doing that, he answers the telephone in the office, or reads the newspaper."

"Are you telling me that there is not enough to do in the Department of Health and Safety?" Helen probed.

"We have work that is a year overdue. But the system is afraid to let anything out without the top guys going over and over it. And Ryan has the reputation of rewriting everything himself. He doesn't trust anyone to do anything."

"Sounds like a pretty conscientious guy," Helen observed. She actually had a pretty good relationship with Ryan James. They seemed to see the same enemies of incompetence in the system. And he was young and anything but a political hack elevated through sheer longevity. Susan's complaints came from a different world, the inner world of administrative bureaucracy. This, Helen did not fully understand. She would listen to Susan politely, even sympathetically, but Helen could never act on such information. It was just not anything she had a feel for.

"Mr. Chairman," James began, "the State Department of Health and Safety is grateful for this opportunity to present testimony on the issue of alleged contamination of Hawaii's home-grown meats and meat products." James was reading from his carefully drafted testimony, designed, Helen believed, to be as dry and unimaginative as possible. Playing it safe was one of those features of committee testimony that Helen hated most. Randall had defended the practice by noting that many a department head had been raked over the coals for language which was more creative than accurate. If there were members of a committee whose goal was to embarrass the department, they would invariably find any indiscretion in the testimony and seize upon it as proof of whatever they hoped to prove. Randall had argued that the fear of being criticized or embarrassed drove the administrative types to adopt an almost unbearable blandness in their official remarks. It was often believed that the less said the better. The result, Helen lamented, was a constant struggle by the committee to pay attention to the droning of department heads in the hope there would be hints of real information or policy.

"As reported to the legislature in our last annual report," read James, knowing they hadn't read it, "the Department of Health and Safety maintains a comprehensive monitoring system to assure the health and safety of Hawaii's citizens. This system is administered by our Office of Toxic Substance Control, which was created by Act 902-84. The purpose of the Office is to carry out the goals of the Act, which include, quote, 'To monitor Hawaii's water, dairy products and meats for the existence of toxic substances; To set standards for the acceptable levels of toxic substances consistent with the requirements for public health; To inform the public of its findings; and to, when necessary, take appropriate actions to correct violations of such standards.'"

Barbara Lum quickly jotted down the main goals of the law. As a generalist she was glad to be reminded of what the law was supposed to accomplish. But she wondered what effect this kind of repetition and lecture had on the legislators themselves. Some, she knew, were lazy and uniformed and needed the reminder. But others, people interested in the issue at hand, could recite the law from memory. As she glanced around the table, she could see heavy eyelids on Melvin Richards and Wayne Davis. The Chairman was playing with a paperclip. Helen Tokugawa was writing a note to Randall Ogawa. Michael Robinson had left the room and was hanging over the railing in a hushed conversation with Ramsey Bingham. The mood of the room was clearly one of boredom and distraction. She wondered if everyone else felt the same thing. *Was this hearing just a meaningless show? Was she being manipulated by both sides to cover a non-event?* Her doubts were somewhat erased by an abrupt comment to the speaker.

"Mr. James," interrupted Patrick Lee, "it is not necessary to recite to this committee the very law it wrote. We do not need a lecture on the law. What we need is your testimony on this issue." Several heads snapped to attention. Patrick Lee was not the sort of person who usually interrupted a witness, let alone criticized their style. He was a content man, and his impatience over Ryan James was more a reflection of the impatience felt by some that the hearing was being deliberately dragged out to deaden any action agenda.

"I'm sorry Senator Lee. I was only trying to put the issue into perspective. Perhaps I should summarize the rest of my remarks," he asked as he glanced at the Chairman. Tanaka would have preferred the calming effect of an extended verbatim reading, but he nodded his grudging approval for James to depart from the text.

"Mr. Chairman, the department is doing its job. It is not an easy job. Science is not as exact as many would want. We review the facts. We try to balance our mandates, which in some cases seem to conflict. We must protect the public from harmful substances, but at the same time we must act only when we have proof to back us up. We cannot shut down an industry just because of a suspicion. Our attorneys tell us that if we act too soon we could be open to a costly law suit. We have a responsibility to act in a manner which does not put the state treasury in jeopardy. I submit to the members of this committee that the department is acting responsibly, and that we have nothing to be ashamed of."

Sandra was surprised at the aggressiveness of this young bureaucrat. He came on strong, with no apologies. He, more than anyone else, Davis felt, needed to be cut down to size - taught a little humility. Ryan James was the sort of fellow older legislators like Davis were bothered by. There some that could be written off as mindless defenders of the status quo. But some, like James, were still salvageable. *If only Ryan could be made to see his prejudices*, Sandra thought. *If only his considerable talents could be channeled not into a circle-the-wagons defense, but into real problem solving.*

Patrick Lee asked with an edge to his voice, "Mr. James, would you respond directly to the testimony of Mr. Logan from the EPA?" To Lee, it was unbelievable that James could defend his department as if Triptathol had never been mentioned.

"Mr. Logan's information is now being evaluated by our department. Until we have had the time to thoroughly analyze his data it would be inappropriate to comment."

Helen could barely contain herself, even if she did bear a grudging appreciation for Ryan James. "You have just heard the result of the Stanford studies, Mr. James. Let us suppose for a moment that your department people were to conclude that his data was correct. What would be the appropriate response to that conclusion," she asked.

"If the data were correct, and that remains to be seen, they we would have to consider whether or not the results warranted a program of monitoring our meats. If the meats were found to contain this substance over a significant period, then were would have to consider controls or even a ban. We would not hesitate to protect the public."

Mr. James," Chairman Tanaka began, "We appreciate the efforts of your department and are confident that the public will be well served. Are there any final questions of Mr. James?" Tanaka was pushing the hearing along, hoping that he could conclude early enough to make it out to his favorite country club for a round of golf with Jim Thompson and Mike Robinson. He was therefore a little surprised when Michael raised his hand to be recognized.

"Mr. James, I understand that the department, even though it is not yet required to do so, is actually carrying out a low profile monitoring and testing program. Is this true?" Robinson enjoyed both praising the department and a probing for information with a question that demonstrated he had done his homework. It was his delight to combine roles for it represented to him the essence of the complexity of legislative life. Helen recognized this from the old days when they worked together in Eastland's office. She could tell he was doing it by the way he cocked his head and raised his left eyebrow. It was one of the sides of Michael, his mastery of the job and the institution that she both admired and feared.

"Yes, Representative Robinson, as a matter of fact, we do have an ongoing effort to sample meat and water from a wide geographical area in the State to determine the scope of possible contamination. We do not normally discuss this effort because it is not scientific, in the true sense. It merely tells us about potential trouble areas where we go in and do more extensive evaluation. In most cases, the warning signs by the preliminary monitoring usually are found to be false alarms."

"Why is that?"

"Because a major problem these days is the contamination of samples by the labs themselves. We are working on statewide standards, but we don't have them yet, so we can never be sure just how reliable tests are. We find that in most cases the traces found in samples were put there by the labs, inadvertently."

"Would it be possible," Michael continued, "to meet with some of your people to take a look at where you have been testing? I'm just curious to know how you do it, for my own background information, as well as assuring some colleagues that you are indeed as thorough as you need to be."

"No problem," answered James. He looked over his shoulder go one of his aides as he said, "I'm sure we can arrange for a meeting with our monitoring project people." As he left the room with his aide, everyone recognized that this brash and intelligent team had done well. He ended his testimony in the best possible way, by promising nitty gritty information to assist the legislators in their awesome decisions. Chairman Tanaka, Jim Thompson, and Melvin Richards were impressed. You didn't have to worry about James handling himself when the heat was on, they concluded. But they also wondered what kind of a foe he could be, and whether or not his loyalties were firm or merely convenient. Michael Robinson was impressed too. He prided himself in mastering 'the system,' and he could recognize those who played the same game. *It was a terrific performance*, he thought, not without a little envy.

Barbara Lum felt depressed. Her professionalism told her that the preceding twenty minutes was unimportant for her story, except to provide some clichéd balance, the pro-forma administrative defense against community emotions. She was unconcerned with the substance of what Ryan had said. What bothered her was that she was a witness to a dance by insiders. She could see the nodding approval on Michael Robinson's young-but-old face, and that approval was not for public service, but for a *performance. Politics and show-biz. It was not a new thing; in fact, it had a certain staleness to it. To be really good at it*, she thought, *you had to learn to take delight in the superficial, the aesthetics of it. And in the process, who knows what was lost.*

She was depressed because she did not share in that inner world of power, a world she had hoped to tap through her media career but which had eluded her. She was saddened that the world she yearned to participate in was less worthy than the players. *Somehow, to be a good professional politician was less than uplifting.* It was not an uncommon disappointment by media people. Their need to be skeptical took its toll on their idealism. The bright ones like Lum, were sensitive enough to wonder which was more artificial, the world they reported on, or the eyes through which they saw it.

Chairman Tanaka was sure that the hearing was over. "Is there anyone else who would like to testify," he asked, confident that the efforts of Helen Tokugawa and her cohorts had fallen flat. Barbara Lum enjoyed the look of surprise and consternation on his face when a dark haired middle aged woman stood up from the back row of seats and asked to be allowed to speak.

The woman, wearing a light blue blouse and dark purple elastic slacks, was visibly nervous, observed Lum. *Was this the mysterious witness the station had been tipped off about?*

Helen and Randall glanced at each other in relief. It had not been easy to locate the author of the letter to Paradise Underwriters that

Eastland had sent over before his death. Mrs. Flora Garcia was not the sort of person to make waves, but since the death of her husband, she had learned to stand up for herself and her four children. Writing a letter complaining to the insurance company would not have been possible without the help of her nephew, who was in law school. It was his idea to send a copy to Senator Eastland, who was known to be investigating pollution of some sort. Only after several hours of coaching and reassurances could Helen and Randall convince Flora to come forward. She had promised to think it over. Helen was not certain she would even show up for the hearing, but she took the gamble and had Betsy Ito phone the KARE TV people.

Flora had with her a slightly wrinkled set of papers she took out of her purse and without looking up or asking permission to begin she took the seat at the end of the long conference table and immediately began reading her statement.

"Dear Senator, and other members of this body," she heard herself speak, and this gave her confidence, even though her voice was weak and reading halting.

"My name is Mrs. Flora Garcia, and a live at 2447 Pilikia Drive, which is next to the old Smithville Plantation, which as you probably know, was taken out of sugar production many years ago. I have four children, Ages 17, 14, 13, and eight. I work at the Barbers Point Vista Hotel and attend Blessed. Damien Church.

"I have come before you today because I am concerned about the health of my children, and the health of other children who live in the area. For many years our family has relied on a private well for our drinking water. For many years this was OK, and the water seemed good. But now, Senators, the water seems not so good. In the last few years all of my children have experienced illness which the doctors could not explain, at first. They would wake up in the middle of the night with cold sweats. They would lose their appetites. And finally, last April, my youngest, Theresa, began losing some of her hair."

Barbara began listening closer, as did Ramsey Bingham.

"Finally the clinic sent some of Theresa's blood and did some tests. They found out that there was some new kind of chemical, I can't remember the name. I sent my Theresa to live with her aunty, and

I wrote a letter to the insurance people. I ask them to test our water and to pay the doctor bills. They have never answered my letter yet. I am here today because I want you people to do something about the chemicals. I want my Theresa and my other children to live a healthy life and to come home. Thank you."

Lum noticed that the Chairman and his friends were quite surprised by this witness, but their reactions were nothing like that of Ramsey Bingham who was sitting near her and who seemed to almost choke when she mentioned the old Smithville Plantation. Michael Robinson also looked like he'd just seen a ghost.

Sandra Shamoto-Burns got the Chairman's attention to begin the questioning. She wanted to reassure Mrs. Garcia, and head off any attempt to discredit her.

"Mrs. Garcia, how long have you lived at your current address?"

"About 15 years, Ma'am."

"You own your house and the land?"

"No, we lease it for 25 years. It's a very affordable arrangement."

"I wonder if you would mind telling us who you lease it from."

"We lease it from the Palaka Produce Company. They own all the land in the area, most of the old Smithville property."

"Do you know anything about this company? Who owns it or runs it?"

"I don't really know much. You see my husband handled all the finances. After he died a man from the company visited and explained that nothing would change. We would just keep sending in the checks. Mr. Wilcox was always very kind to us. He even sent us a turkey for Christmas that first year after Thomas died."

Ramsey Bingham quickly made his way towards the door. Barbara Lum would have followed but she was busy writing down *Palaka Produce Company* and *Mr. Wilcox*.

"Thank you Mrs. Garcia."

Michael Robinson was next. "Mrs. Garcia, did the doctor know what was causing your children's illnesses?"

"No sir."

"He was not able to identify what was wrong, then?"

"No, except that when he told us about the chemical in Theresa' blood."

"Did he know for certain that the chemicals were related to her illness?"

"I don't know. All I know is that he thought they might be the cause, sir."

"So as of today, Mrs. Garcia, you really don't have any evidence that your problems have anything to do with chemical pollution, do you?"

"No sir, I guess not," she answered, regretting that she had allowed herself to be talked into coming down to the capitol in the first place.

"Mrs. Garcia, why did you come today? Did someone ask you to come?"

"Well," Flora glanced at Helen, uncertain whether or not their meeting was something to be kept in the strictest confidence or not. Helen decided not to let Mrs. Garcia serve as a target.

"Mr. Chairman, Helen broke in, "I requested that Mrs. Garcia come forward when I learned of her problem. I felt it was pertinent to the committee's inquiry. It may be that the apparent contamination of her well involves the same toxic substance we have discovered in our meat. Mrs. Garcia, I'm sure we all appreciate you taking your valuable time to testify today."

Michael Robinson was disappointed that Helen's explanation had not allowed him to imply that Garcia had been coached by a biased tutor. His disappointment however, was nothing compared to his irritation that someone like Mrs. Garcia had appeared at all. It was not part of his preferred scenario. It did not fit into his self-image of being in control.

Jim Thompson felt obliged to press the relevance of the issue. "Mrs. Garcia, can you offer this committee any information which relates your allegedly contaminated well to the issue of Triptathol in Hawaii's meats?"

"I'm not sure I understand the question, sir.'

"My question," Thompson was getting impatient, "is what the hell are you here for?"

Flora looked at the Chairman pleadingly, and although he would have loved to let Thompson continue, even he recognized that Helen's explanation made the issue not one of citizen vs. Committee, but one member's judgment vs. another's. "Senator Tokugawa has covered that point, Jim."

"One final clarification, Mr. Chairman," Patrick Lee said. "Mrs. Garcia, just one final question. You said the land you live on is owned by the Palaka Produce Company, and they also own all the land adjacent to your property?"

"That is correct."

"Thank you Mr. Chairman, no further questions."

Chairman Tanaka was anxious to end the whole business. Golf was now out of the question. Mrs. Garcia had let the cat – just which cat he was not sure – but a dangerous cat – out of the bag. He knew things were bad when Ramsey Bingham could not stand to watch any longer.

"If there are no further witnesses, I would like to conclude this hearing. In summary, we have heard from Senator Shamoto-Burns, who provided us with her figures related to meat in Hawaii; Mr. Logan of the EPA; Mr. Soong from the Sugar Planters; Mrs. Thelma Winters of the Leeward Community Action Coalition; Mr. James from our State Department of Health & Safety; and Mrs. Garcia. We have explored this question from the perspective of the Federal Government, the State Government, the private sector, the community and individual citizens. I'm sure all would agree that such diversity represents a thorough consideration of the issues at hand. Mr. James has assured us that further test results will be forwarded to this committee. Until that information is available, this Committee is adjourned."

As the gavel struck, Barbara was up and moving quickly toward Mrs. Garcia, but the crowd got in the way. Helen intercepted the star interviewee and escorted her into a nearby office. It was Randall's idea that further contact with the media might do more harm than good. "Let Lum do some digging herself," he had scribbled in a note to Helen.

Patrick was not very satisfied with the way the hearing had gone. *It was true that both Thelma Winters and Flora Garcia had focused attention on how the State was not handling the problem of chemical pollution, but the rest of the hearing was a draw. Chair Tanaka had been in full control. At times he conveyed the impression that the hearing was just a waste of time. If Barbara Lum had not shown up no public record of the hearing would have been made. And her report still had to make the deadline for the evening news. Who knows what the final impression might be? If Lum's angle is just another example of political infighting, the whole purpose was lost,* he thought.

CHAPTER SIX

It was an austere suite overlooking the most fashionable business district of London. The day's late afternoon fog mostly obscured the view of Big Ben as it struck 4 pm, further irritating the man waiting for a call that was already twenty minutes late. He sipped a scotch on the rocks as he once again reviewed the report before him, detailing actuarial tables, benefits paid, investment income, and other data used to measure the insurance business.

Carleton Brent was just one small cog in the London insurance machine, but he took pride in being one of their most effective enforcers. He was financially secure for life because he had made a successful career out of being unsympathetic to any interest that did not maximize the influence and profits of *The Empire*, as it was known in the trade. He had translated this into three piece suits, expensive cars, a second home in the country, and three strife-ridden marriages. He ate at the best restaurants, hired the most beautiful and eager-to-please secretaries, and drank the best scotch whenever he waited for late phone calls.

"Mr. Brent," sang Stephani over the intercom, using just enough breathiness to remind her boss of their temporary delay in their planned liaison, "your call from Hawaii is on line two." Brent allowed himself the luxury of a moment's reflection on Stephani's enthusiastic body before he reluctantly picked up the receiver.

"You're twenty minutes late."

"Sorry, but it's only six in the morning here and..."

"What have you done to solve our problem," snapped Brent, using his irritation over the delay in his afternoon frolic with Stephani to harshen his response. Brent was the master at long distance hardball.

"Well, we still have some difficulty. Our people are doing the best we can to prevent public disclosure. We are making progress, Mr. Brent, but we need more time."

"I don't have to tell you that any breach of security over this and we cancel your policy. You know what that means, it means you are effectively out of business."

"Mr. Brent, those of us in the chemical industry appreciate your tolerance," said the caller, trying to control his contempt for Brent. *These guys are going to squeeze until there is nothing left*, he thought. On the mainland, more and more firms, unable to find reinsurance, were resorting to alliances with the underworld to solve their problems. So far, Hawaii was clean, but if Brent pushed too hard, there might not be any choice. He hated having to toady to this English bastard he'd never met, but it was the only way Ramsey Bingham could survive. "We know you've been patient, and all we ask is to extend the deadline just a little longer. We are confident we can contain the crisis."

Brent loved the perversity of these long distance shake-downs, as he called them. "I think it is time we sent one of our contractors out to size things up. If there is no visible progress, or if things deteriorate, well, you know our policy."

Brent listened to his client with distraction, as Stephani entered the office and began to run her fingers through his well-groomed hair. Her perfume alone was enough to excite him. Her hands began to wander but he pushed her away gently. It was essential to maintain his composure on the line, especially as his client began to list the specific measures that had been taken. Brent was a bit annoyed, for it was his habit not to be informed as to how his clients twisted the law to meet his demands.

"I'll expect a call from you in two weeks. I'll expect progress." He hung up an allowed himself to give in to Stephani's impatience.

***

Senator Bobby Martin had found no appetite to attend the hearing. He knew they expected him, but he also knew that his presence would probably have little or no impact. The only concern would be if they took a vote, and the Chair assured him that would not happen.

Instead, he stayed home and tended his small garden. It was a lazy day. He had chatted with the mailman when he delivered the usual collection of junk mail, *Time*, and a few assorted letters. It was not until after lunch that he settled down in his den to look over the day's offerings.

One letter he overlooked at first. It had no return address, but he recognized the handwriting. He glanced over his shoulder to make sure his wife Christine or the kids were not around. His throat was suddenly dry, his palms clammy. He stared at the envelope on his desk for a few minutes, imagining what he would find in it, and fantasizing what he hoped to find.

At last he observed his hand reaching for it. He watched as his fingers poked at the open slot at the top and ripped the envelop down its side. A single, hand-written note emerged. He took a deep breath and unfolded the letter. He glanced around one more time, and got up and closed the door to his study, even though the afternoon sun was bright and the room was stuffy.

"Dear B." it began, in the recognizable style of the author, who always addressed letters with the first initial only. As Bobby Martin's eyes moved quickly down the page, his heart leaped for joy and excitement. Could he believe it? Was Bill Wilcox really acknowledging their special relationship?

His mind focused on the key phrases… "Please be part of my life…I need you…share our joys together…I long to hold you in the night…"

For years Bobby Martin had led a secret life. His homosexuality was firmly hidden in his closet, disguised with a full family life and his public image in the straight political world. He had taken every precaution, he felt, in his infrequent liaisons. They were rare, for he longed not for a passionate encounter, but a friendship-love relationship. His attentions were often drawn to men around the capitol, but he had never dared to approach any of them.

Now, unbelievably, a man he had secretly been attracted to was approaching him. Their relationship had not developed in the best of circumstances. Bill Wilcox, somehow, somewhere, had found out about Bobby's other life. In fact, Bill was using that knowledge to actually blackmail him.

First, Wilcox had demanded his vote on the sugar bill, which Bobby had unconvincingly excused to his friends as a result of personal confusion. Then, and more seriously, was his suspiciously timely illness which deprived Helen of a key vote on the bill to establish a department of the environment. Bobby knew that sooner or later he would have to come forward. He simply could not allow himself to be so manipulated. He developed severe acid indigestion, and sought medical help in fear of an ulcer. He was especially attentive to his family, hoping that when the time came he would be able to explain his other life without hurting them too much. His guilt was enormous, but not as intimidating as his fear. His life in politics could be ruined.

To Bobby, the letter was tender and revealing. Big Bill Wilcox was exposing his soul. Bobby could tell that once he did there would be no turning back for him. The note ended with a promise to contact him soon. Bobby let his hand with the letter drop to his lap. Gradually his shock and euphoria gave way to anticipation: *When will he call? Would he dare call here? Will he arrange a special place to meet? Will he just want to talk"* Oh Bill, *I know we can have a special relationship, in spite of all that has happened. I know someone else is forcing to play the role of the blackmailer, probably Ramsey Bingham, that S.O.B.*

***

Almost at the same time that day, Betsy Ito, still serving as a kind of office manager for the deceased Eastland Bridges, was going through letters which arrived daily, automatically, from distant offices in the governmental system. They were sent not because they thought Bridges was alive, they were just sent because there was a legislative office, a mailing list, a center of power and, hopefully, of interest. They kept coming even if the person ceased to exist. Some letters, however, were addressed to Mrs. Bridges. Those she kept in a special pile, and delivered to Mei-ling once a week. One envelope, however, was addressed to her.

She recognized the bold handwriting immediately. Bill Wilcox sent her dozens of small notes, some attached to flowers, and she had grown to anticipate his manly scrawl. She quickly opened it and began reading with eager attention. It was not what she had expected.

It began abruptly with no greeting, and was terse and cold.

"Meeting with BM arranged soon. Will give him the report to be planted in PU files clearing well of pollution. Anticipate no trouble, as he

is frightened. Am keeping in touch with actions of Bridges people, HT, etc., by cultivating relationship with B. Ito, who confides in me. Taking steps to sell off Smithville property to a subsidiary to make tracing difficult. Please advise on appropriate price. I will be in touch." Signed, "B. Wilcox."

She did not understand what was written. She looked again at the envelope to make sure it was addressed to her. It was, and in Bill's unmistakable hand. Her tear-filled eyes returned to that awful phrase: *Am keeping in touch with actions of Bridges people, HT, etc., by cultivating relationship with B. Ito, who confides in me.*

Betsy was hurt. *All this time, could it be that he was just manipulating me? It was all a ruse? I was just a pawn? How could I have been so stupid? I thought he cared for me.*

She crushed the letter into a crinkled ball between her two hands and threw it awkwardly at the waste basket, not caring that it missed its mark. She sobbed; she cried. She was beside herself with pain and anger. She paced up and down the office. She tried to compose herself with a cup of coffee, but it was no consolation.

Betsy Ito threw herself down on the small sofa in the reception area and stared at the office walls. She did not see the public art work Eastland had been issued, and which he agreed to hang in the absence of anything better. Instead, she saw only the face of Bill Wilcox. She saw his twinkling eyes, his large hands, his shyness. And she heard his charming voice. It was all too much to take.

After some time, she began to realize that the letter was obviously not intended for her. She mustered her anger and her courage and retrieved the wadded paper for further inspections. It was obviously a report of some sort, and she did not like the tone of it. Repressing her emotions, she began to analyze the rest of the contents. Something about planting a report, as if to falsify something. Something about someone being frightened. Obviously, if she were a source of information, it must be information connected with Bridges, and with Helen, the reference to "H.T.", Helen Tokugawa. *Was she an unwitting leak in the system?* She searched her memory for evidence of what she might have said that could be used against her boss. Nothing came to mind, only Bill Wilcox's charm, and now his betrayal.

Unable to make sense out of this turn of events, Betsy vowed she must seek help. She reapplied her makeup to her tear washed faced, and left the office seeking her confident, Helen Tokugawa.

***

Bill Wilcox hung over the bar and nursed his beer. He was feeling depressed again, partly because he disliked being used for the dirty work of Ramsey Bingham, and partly because he could feel the extra pounds he'd been putting on lately.

It was one of the oldest bars in Honolulu, and the ancient wooden bar rail and ceiling had that sour, musty odor to it – years of alcohol, dust and smoke. The ceiling fan cast only a feint shadow on the pool table because the overhead lights were dim and dirty, barely giving off more light than the rays of the mid-morning sun that flooded the open door. It was Wilcox's favorite place to feel sorry for himself.

Ten minutes late, as usual, Bobby Martin peered into the dark room from the sidewalk, unable to make out where he was walking. If Wilcox had bothered to look, he would have noticed that Martin's face was filled with both fear and excitement. He made no sign of recognition when Martin stood next to him and said, "Bill, I'm here."

Martin did not know what to expect. He ordered a beer and sat nervously for what seemed like a half hour before Wilcox turned to begin their conversation. "Sorry about the elegant surroundings, Senator, but what we have to say…"

"No problem, Bill. I understand. You have to remember I've been living like this for years, afraid to be seen. I know how hard it must have been for you to come at all. But believe me, the first step is the hardest."

"Look Martin, stop your babbling and listen."

"No Bill, you listen to me. This is my territory, and I can help you through it. I admire you Bill, not only because of my feelings for you, but because of your courage. I know what it took to write this note, believe me, I know." He removed the love letter from his pocket and slapped it on the bar face up. "And I want you to know there is nothing to be ashamed of. People like us can share a great deal, Bill. I can show you…"

Wilcox's eyes flashed at the note and instantly went into shock as he recognized what had happened.

"People like us? What the hell are you babbling about? Gimmie that note." Unable to believe the depth of his blunder, Wilcox again scanned the handwritten note… *"Please be part of my life…I need you…share our joys together…I long to hold you in the night…"*

Martin was nearly knocked off his seat as Wilcox lunged for the men's room holding his mouth. He was still bewildered when Wilcox came back wiping his face, obviously having lost his breakfast and white as a ghost.

Wilcox towered over Martin as he grabbed Bobby's lapels and lifted his torso closer to his angry scowl.

"Look here you God Damned wimp. You forget this letter. It's a mistake. It's for somebody else. Don't you ever, ever even thin…" Wilcox was shaking with rage and embarrassment.

"But Bill, I thought…"

'Shaddup. You listen. Your orders are to get into the files and replace the Garcia claim letter with this report. And you better be sure it's done, or your wife, God knows why she married one of you, your wife and your loyal voters will find out just what kind of a deviant you are. Do you understand?" He shoved the falsified report into Martin's hands.

Martin, now aware that Wilcox was not a future lover but just his blackmailer, could only stare unbelievingly at Wilcox. He was speechless. Assuming that Martin had gotten the message, and anxious to be alone to sort out and comprehend what had happened, Wilcox left his love-sick prey at the bar and disappeared into the glaring sunlight of the open door.

Wilcox's mind was reeling with fear. It leapt from one horrible realization to another…*Martin, the wrong note…who got the blackmail note? Did I send the wrong one to Betsy? What about Ramsey? Is this going to blow the whole cover-up? Maybe I should leave town.* He walked twice around the block through Chinatown before he found his car parked in front of the same bar.

Shaken by the long hoped-for liaison which had blown up in his face, Bobby Martin quickly paid for both drinks and left for his insurance office with the phony report. As he passed through the door, a lanky figure in the dark corner booth rose and moved silently to the bar with his knapsack. When the bartender turned his back to get change, Stephen Sinclair deftly placed both beer glasses into his bag, careful not to smudge any finger prints. As his rode home in his "72 white Volvo, he pondered how he would use the evidence he was sure he would find.

CHAPTER SEVEN

"There must be a good explanation for what happened," said Helen, but not really believing it. As she drove past the Waikiki Aquarium towards the beachfront hotel opposite Kapiolani Park, she knew it would not be easy consoling Betsy Ito.

"I was such a fool, Helen. He must have been playing me for a stupid middle aged…"

"Stop it Betsy. I'm not going to waste my time listening to you run yourself down." Helen pulling into one of the slanted stalls near the well-known fountain opposite the hotel. "What we've got to do is to try and figure out what that note means. It's part of a bigger puzzle. And I have the feeling that Wilcox is being manipulated too." They walked across the one-way street lined with tall iron wood trees and entered the pleasant open-air cocktail lounge overlooking the beach. The sun was setting and it was the perfect time to unwind and sort out the world. Betsy and Helen had a tradition. If something was bothering one of them, or if something was happening that needed understanding, they would come to this charming place, where the trade winds covered their private conversation.

After ordering their drinks, Betsy felt compelled to avoid the pain of the betrayal by filling Helen in on office business that might concern her. Helen listened patiently, knowing that this was Betsy's way of building up her courage.

"Oh, by the way," Betsy said, raising her head, trying to appear upbeat and matter of fact, "Wayne Davis called yesterday. He was looking for a copy of your Master's Thesis you said you'd loan him. He said you thought Eastland had a copy. You were right, I found it in the file cabinet and sent it on. You were out so I just…'

"You sent him what?"

"You know, that MA paper on politics in Hawaii, the one Wayne…"

"Betsy, I never talked to Wayne about that paper. It was nothing I wanted circulated." Helen was visibly upset, and this further confused Betsy, who was not feeling good about herself in the first place. Helen's eyes briefly flashed with anger, an emotion seldom shown to her good friend Betsy. She was immediately aware of her own reaction, and that this was not the time to come down on Betsy.

"I hope I've not…"

"Betsy, don't' worry. But you've got to be more careful. There is something strange about this, because I've never given anyone a copy except Eastland. Only my advisor at the UH would know, and perhaps a few other students at the time. But I am puzzled why Wayne would know about it in the first place, and then lie about it in the second place." Helen was beginning to feel a little paranoid.

"What's, what's wrong with this paper, Helen?" asked Betsy, trying to control he emotions by being serious and analytical.

"Betsy, you probably remember that when I first came to work for Eastland I was filled with political theories and no experience. I was especially into Marxism and class conflict. I wasn't a Marxist or a communist or anything like that, but their basic way of viewing society was very appealing. It is really Hegel that advances those ideas." She noticed that Betsy was not quite following her. "Well, anyway, my MA thesis was a class-conscious analysis of Hawaiian politics. It was an academic exercise, and, academically, it was not all that bad. But the general public, the general reader would never understand. It is the sort of paper that someone, if he were your enemy, could use against you.'

There was a long silence as each sipped their drinks and pretended to watch the sunset. Suddenly the purpose of their meeting had shifted from one of consolation to one of minimizing damages. Helen forced herself to concentrate on the contents of Betsy's letter, and the unexplainable behavior of Wayne Davis.

"Helen, I know I'm not the brightest…"

"Betsy, stop it."

"I just want to say, and don't interrupt me young lady, I have a right to say this. I just want to say that I would never do anything to hurt you. And now it looks like I'm somehow involved in at least two crazy things, Bill's letter and your paper. What I want you to know is that whatever I can do to help you find out what's going on, I'm ready."

"I appreciate that. I really do. We can start by going over everything you might remember about the last time you saw Bill." Helen and Betsy spend nearly two hours in intense conversation, both of them taking notes. Betsy was impressed again with how thorough Helen was, and how she had an eye for detail. Helen was impressed with how certain people had zeroed in on Betsy for purposes yet unclear. Someone was playing for keeps.

Shortly after 9 o'clock, Betsy and Helen crossed the street past the fountain and headed for Helen's car. The street was well lit, and the tall trees created swaying shadows that were both romantic and foreboding. Neither saw the tall figure move quickly from the fountain, intent on intercepting them before they got to the car. Neither noticed him dash behind a station wagon as the lights of a passing taxi cruised by. They safely drove off unaware of the blue eyes fixed on them from behind.

***

Michael had known that Helen had written her MA paper filled with the rhetoric of the left. It was all she talked about when they worked side by side for Eastland Bridges. He knew that she could not resist exploring those issues that every practicing politician knows are too hot to discuss publically, or are too easily warped by the media. It was almost too easy getting a copy. Davis, his secret ally, was beautiful the way he charmed Betsy out of Eastland's copy. It was just a hunch.

"He probably has a copy, Wayne. Why not assume he has? Tell Betsy…" Wayne knew just what to say. Betsy was a trusting person, especially since the death of Eastland. She went out of her way to help those she thought had been close to her boss. It was a way of vicariously serving a man who she would never serve Again.

Michael instantly recognized the damaging parts of Helen's paper, carefully using the yellow magic marker as he lounged in his Nuuanu apartment drinking a vodka tonic. Most pleasing was the recognition that he had always been right about openness. "Never tell people what you really think," he had once preached to Helen. *Of course she never listened. She was too smart for her own good. Her paper was actually pretty readable, and accurate if he did say so himself. Helen was brighter than he, but he was wiser, he told himself. Sure, she had risen to the Senate, but that was sheer luck: a fluke in reapportionment creating an empty seat, the retirement of an incumbent. In the long run, I'll be the one who survives,* he told himself.

***

It did not take Barbara Lum long to discover that Palaka Produce was a holding company that owned both the Sandwich Isle Chemical Corporation and the old Smithville Plantation lands. She sat in a darkened corner of the Constitutional Inn, not far from the TV station. It was a popular hangout for media people, especially newspaper reporters, who she preferred to her own kind, and politicians. The owner had cultivated the political establishment over the years, and lured the average citizen with autographed pictures of celebrities covering the wall.

Her friend Tom listened patiently as she laid out the basic elements of her story. She liked to bounce things off him before taking it to the station. As a non-journalist, he had the eyes, ears and sensibilities of the man on the street, or so she thought.

Palaka owns Sandwich and Smithville, she explained. Smithville resident complains about toxic wastes, abandoned land. Chemicals.

"Obviously, one angle could be that Sandwich somehow was dumping stuff on the old plantation," said Tom, trying to sound as if the puzzle was easily solved and they could go home. He had other things on his mind and didn't want Barbara to get either too wound up or too drunk. In either case, she would not be in the mood.

"It may be obvious to you, but my news director won't let me say it until I have proof, and until the story leads somewhere," she said as she took another swig of her draft. Tom rolled his eyes. He'd been living with Barbara for six months and they enjoyed each other's company enormously, except that her job seemed to consume more of her attention than he did.

"Did you check into Sandwich's Board of Directors?" Tom asked, now resigned to an evening of journalism and investigation.

"You'll never believe who I found. None other than Representative Michael Robinson! A full-fledged member of the Board of Directors of one of the most powerful holding companies in Hawaii."

"Isn't he one of the younger ones?" Tom tried to avoid memorizing the local political stars, just to keep a distance between his private life with Barbara and her professional involvements. She appreciated the effort but it irritated her to always have to explain who people were. It slowed down her story telling.

"Young, but not necessarily inexperienced. He used to work for Eastland Bridges, along with Senator Helen Tokugawa. You've got to wonder how someone just starting out, so to speak, could get to such a position. You've got to ask yourself, why would they appoint him to such a position?"

"Maybe he's just there for window dressing. You know, just like the bank often hires legislators for community relations. They really are not part of the banking management team, but they are seen as useful when lobbying time comes."

"What you are saying is true, but it's not easy being a legislator."

"Getting soft on the guys you cover, huh?" Tom chided her on a sticky professional point. Reporters always worried about getting too close to the inner circle and losing their objectivity.

"I'm not soft on anyone, Tom, you know that. "It's just that "$17,000 a year isn't much to live on, and not very many businesses are willing to hire a guy for eight months a year, even if there are benefits PR wise."

"I have to admit I wouldn't be willing to do it for that amount of pay. Must be demeaning, really, to earn less than most college grads just coming out."

"That's why they take these crummy jobs, they have no choice. And the business community keeps wanting to keep the legislature as part time. Attorneys, insurance people, a few other jobs, seem to work well with the lifestyle. But not everyone has skills easily sellable. They're mostly all generalists. I guess that's why we elect them. We don't want a specialist who is controlled by one sector of the community."

"Back to the story. So Robinson's in on it you think?"

"I don't know. It would be a hell of a story. Legislator tied to chemical sickness…something like that. But I don't have any real proof, and I can't just go after someone without knowing if they are involved."

"So call Robinson and see what he says."

"No answer. Three days, and the secretary said he's not in and she doesn't know when he'll be back. I doubt it. He's just avoiding me. But that could be because he's mad about the last interview. The way I edited it. He felt it made him sound too critical of the House leadership and he didn't like that."

"Who else do you think is involved? Any other legislators?"

"Hey, don't jump. We don't even know if Robinson is really involved. Like you said, he could be just a name they added for the prestige, you know, not really a functioning member of the board. He might not even know what companies Palaka owns."

"Got any leads?"

"Not really. Just one crazy call from some private investigator named Sinclair. Wants to meet me tomorrow. Says he's got something I might be interested in about toxic wastes. Meeting for lunch."

"Let's get out of here. I love to hear you talk about your work because you get so animated, but I hate to hear the same thing over and over. D'ya mind?"

"I'm ready. And Tom, this time I'm not too tipsy for you know what." She shoved the napkin with her notes on it into her purse and they swayed arm in arm out into the parking lot – Tom thinking about getting home fast – his companion thinking about giving Helen Tokugawa a call first thing in the morning.

***

Stephen Sinclair walked nervously along Beretania Street toward Bishop. Downtown Honolulu emptied out at noon with thousands of secretaries and professionals seeking a quick lunch and a stroll through their favorite stores. Sinclair always thought of himself as an urban person and could understand why the hub of Honolulu became a ghost town after dark. That was the financial area – Bishop and King, Bishop and Merchant, the center of pacific business for more than a century. Just a few blocks away was a different story. What was left of old Chinatown blended with the sleaze of Hotel Street – the red light district. Many of the older buildings were being refurbished as office space with a 19th century touch. The tradeoff, however, was that they were effectively out of commission for the evening.

He was hoping to get to a small restaurant down a narrow alley before the crowd really got rolling. It was 11:45 and he wanted to secure a table away from the door for his meeting with reporter Barbara Lum. She had wanted Chinese food, but Sinclair was not in the mood for a noisy restaurant. He wanted a place where he could whisper and be heard.

Lum arrived almost at the same time. He recognized her from KARE broadcasts and quickly introduced himself. He felt her eyes suspiciously "case" him, and that she was silently demanding that her valuable time be well spent. He allowed her the pleasure of superiority – what he had to say was too important.

"I appreciate you taking time, I wouldn't have called if it weren't important," he began apologetically as he looked over the menu. As sophisticated as he thought he was, he still was a bit star-struck with a TV personality. Barbara was terrific looking in person, he thought. She noticed that she had made a good impression, which is just what she had wanted. It gave her the edge in face to face meetings. *People really were intimidated when you overdressed and wore just the right amount of jewelry and make-up*, she thought.

"Not at all. What can I do for you? You said something about chemicals."

"I'm a private investigator. Before we begin, I need to have an understanding that everything I say, *everything*, is off the record, anonymous, deep background, whatever the term.'

"I wish you had told me before," she flashed, pretending to be irritated. "But as long as we are here you might as well tell me. I agree. Off the record."

"I have information regarding the death of Eastland Bridges."

"I thought you wanted to talk about chemicals."

"I do. It's all related. You see, a man who works for the Palaka Produce Corporation was in Bridges' office the day he died. May even be responsible."

"How do you know this? I thought the conclusion was that Bridges fell and hit his head. The investigation apparently showed no evidence to the contrary." She looked at him wondering if she had another paranoid on her hands. She instinctively glanced at the pathway to the door just to see if she could exit gracefully. She knew what kind of scene some of these kooks might cause.

"They were sloppy. They had no reasons to suspect anything. I was hired by someone who does have reasons. I can prove that a certain William Wilcox was in Bridges' office the day of his death. I've got the fingerprints on a glass that was in the wastebasket. I matched them with another set of prints I saw Wilcox leave on a glass in a bar just a few days Ago. They are identical."

"Have you gone to the police?"

"I'm not sure I can. For one thing, they would want to know how I got into Bridges' office. I'm not at liberty to reveal that. At least not yet. And if the police didn't believe my story, how could I prove that the prints I took came from the two glasses? You see, I work alone, quietly, for my clients. They want it that way. They open some doors, but they want to remain in the background."

"So why do you come to me?" Barbara asked automatically, as her mind turned over the implications.

"You know why. You can make the connections, conduct the investigation. With this lead you know where to look. You can unravel the case," he said, with no particular conviction in his voice. Lum was not convinced either.

"I think your client sent you to me. I think someone wants this exposed in the media. Am I right?"

"You could be. I admit that it would be valuable to have it made public. But not until the whole story hangs together. My client is still probing, too. The advantage of going to you, to be candid, is that the press is often granted a certain immunity with respect to sources. *'We have discovered, by means of a confidential source, that certain fingerprints in Bridges' office may belong to an employee of a company that Bridges was investigating.'* It is perfectly natural for you to refuse to reveal your source. It's different for me. I could lose my license if my methods are found to be illegal. It is much safer all around." He looked into her heavily shaded eyes, searching for a glimmer of acceptance. He wanted to be convinced that she was willing to pick up the ball and run with it.

They fell silent as their lunch was delivered by the waitress. Lum used the break to review the facts of the case and make a snap judgment about Sinclair's credibility.

"So you are not working for an attorney," she said casually as she shoved a forkful of salad into her mouth, slightly smudging her dark lipstick. She wanted Sinclair to know that she was smart enough to recognize that if he had worked for an attorney, that attorney could claim attorney-client privilege. The attorney could be a middle man between the real client and this reporter. Sinclair smiled sheepishly and nodded that she was correct, pleased that she had understood the implications of his dilemma. He wanted her to believe that she had extracted information that he had not intended to give her.

"Do you have more for me?"

"Not now, but I hope to soon. I can point you in several directions. At the same time, I'll be doing my own digging. I know you are a tough researcher. I've seen your stories on TV. If you don't mind me saying so, you're a pretty good reporter. I respect your talents. I think we can work together well," he pushed, feeling that he now had the upper hand. He was in control, as long as he avoided looking at her well filled Chinese blouse.

"Do you have the prints?"

He removed a manila envelope from his brief case and handed it to her. She smiled when she saw he had given her copies and not the originals. But it was clear enough, she thought, for her contact at the police station to determine whether or not the prints were the same.

"It's a deal," she said abruptly. Without finishing lunch, she rose and told him to meet her at the same place next week to compare notes. If he didn't have anything more by then, she would be inclined to terminate their relationship. He nodded as she walked out of the door. *Helen was right,* Sinclair thought. *Lum could not resist having an inside track for what could turn out to be the story of the decade.* It was the 'Pulitzer Prize' syndrome, she said. They both hoped that Lum would dig up more information than they had come across.

***

Ramsey Bingham and Michael Robinson stood at the stone wall overlooking Kaneohe, Oahu. The famous Pali Lookout was windy as usual, but the day was perfect. To the left, far above were the tall cliffs from which King Kamehameha's enemies had jumped – or were pushed – to their deaths in the 1790s. Just below, about 100 feet, were the remains of the original old Pali road as it wound its way down to the windward side of Oahu. It was a safe place to meet, for conversations were made private by the accelerated trade winds.

"Wilcox has done it again," Michael began. "First, he botched the job at the capitol. Now he sends the wrong notes to the wrong people. We've got to put a lid on him. Do you know what was in the one I got?"

Ramsey Bingham leaned over the railing, he eyes looked out on a spectacular view of Kaneohe Bay, its bright blue waters speckled with white sailboats, but he did not see anything. He was thinking of Wilcox, searching for something that was salvageable.

"He still is useful. He still can perform useful functions. You said in your phone call he met with Martin, gave him the report. There needs to be a follow-up to put more pressure on the man," Bingham said, speaking slowly, ponderously. He struggled to put together the preferred scenario.

"Somehow, you don't sound like you mean it."

Bingham looked at Michael and nodded. He was unprepared to reveal the enormous pressure he was getting from London, or the appearance of their local contractor which Bingham was forced to provide reports to.

"Perhaps we should get Wilcox out of the state," suggested the young legislator, thinking of his growing vulnerability, and the unknown implications of the mix-up with the letters. "Send him to one of our overseas operations where he can be conveniently unreachable by any authorities or reporters. We have operations in Papua New Guinea. We can send him there."

"Have you gotten any flak over the letter or anything else," asked Bingham, cutting to the real meaning of Michael's suggestion.

"A few calls from a reporter, the one who got me in trouble with the leadership. I don't know what she wants, but I don't intend to find out. There is good news, however, we were able to get ahold of a very interesting paper written by Senator Helen Tokugawa. You should read it Ramsey, it's dynamite. Just the leverage we might use to put a damper on Helen's aggressive pursuit of the puritan spirit," he said, chuckling to himself.

Bingham's mood darkened. He had cultivated Michael Robinson because he was bright and willing to cooperate. He had even grown to like this young, ambitious politician. But Robinson's flaw was that he was too eager to take the low road, to grasp for the expedient. Bingham was not opposed to that at all, but if you were too eager, you were apt to make mistakes. He now considered the decision to let Michael handle the Wilcox-Martin operation as a mistake. Michael had not been careful with Wilcox, and as a result, someone, somewhere, had incriminating evidence of a cover-up.

"I'll take care of it right way," said Michael. "I'll make sure that Wilcox is out of the state by the end of the week.

"You'd better call him soon, give him time to prepare," advised Bingham, thinking that Big Brother in London might insist on other arrangements. Bingham wanted to be in control at all times, to the extent he could maintain control. That is why he decided not to involve Michael in the details of the insurance problem. Michael would know something, but not everything. That was the safest way, thought Bingham.

Separately, they walked to their cars and drove off.

***

Helen Tokugawa and Randall Ogawa held their eyes to the floor in respect. There was nothing to be said as they pondered what Bobby Martin had just told them. Martin had carried around the doctored report given him by Wilcox for two days before deciding what to do.

In spite of the shocking implications of what Martin said, both Helen and Randall were more in awe of Martin's courage. Here was a man they had written off as weak and unreliable. And now he was putting his career, his reputation, and his friendships on the line.

"Bobby," Helen whispered, "we had no idea. It must have been horrible for you, this last year. But, and I know I'm speaking for Randall too, you're doing the right thing. We only wish you could have told us earlier."

"I wish I had too. Somehow, I thought it would all disappear. Somehow, I hoped that what they were forcing me to do was a small matter, good for their profits but of no harm to anyone. Now it is clear that this is the big time, and I can't help but think it is all tied in with Eastland."

"The implications are there," began Randall, anxious to shift the emotional confession to an analysis of the unfolding conspiracy. "We are just beginning to get a picture of what has been going on. Robinson's involved. Wilcox is involved. Your insurance company is involved."

"Bobby, how far are you willing to go with this?" Helen asked.

"I'm ready to come clean. I've already told my wife and family. They took it hard. My wife is upset, naturally. We don't really know where we go from here, in terms of our relationship. But she has promised that she'll support me at least until this ordeal is over. She'll stick by my side. After it's over, then we will sit down and talk about the future."

"You're a lucky man, Bobby," Randall said. "For the time being, I wonder if it might be wise to act as if you were still sweating the blackmail. Don't let on that you have told anyone. It might be useful for others to assume everything is still going according to their plans. What do you think Helen?"

"I agree. Bobby, you've got to convince Wilcox that you are still afraid of being exposed, and that no one can find out about your... situation."

"I understand. No problem. What else? I'm relying on you guys for advice."

"The second thing, and this is crucial for you legally, is to contact the police."

"The police?"

"Yes. I know a detective. He's the one who did the investigation of Eastland's death. You should go to him with the evidence of blackmail. Let him begin his investigation quietly. You'll need corroboration. Tell him I'm willing to talk, too."

"You? How are you involved? What can you tell him?"

Helen glanced at Randall. He nodded.

"Just before Eastland died he sent me an envelope. It was a report from your company which contained the letters of complaint from Mrs. Garcia. It was the first inkling that there might have been something going on the Smithville land. It might be significant that Eastland had that information. Clearly, Wilcox and his people wanted to purge the files of those documents. That's why they were blackmailing you. So I can testify that Eastland had uncovered something. Perhaps there's a link to his death." She thought it wise not to add what Steven Sinclair had found about the fingerprints.

Martin got up from his seat and began pacing the floor, trying to think out loud. He felt he was on the verge of making some connections but could not quite put it together. Helen and Randall let him pace, unwilling to reveal all they knew. "Remove the files," he said. "Replace the reports with a phony one absolving the company of any responsibility. Blackmail. Chemicals and Smithville. Eastland knew. He knew. He had a copy. Did Wilcox know about that copy? Chemicals in the beef…somewhere it all fits together."

"We'll do it eventually, Bobby," said Helen soothingly. The important thing now is to go promptly to the police. The detective's name is Byron Park. He's familiar with the case. He'll talk to you. Your job is to help them build a case against Wilcox and his superiors. Who is behind it? We've got to consider the danger of scaring off the real target. Understand?"

"Don't worry. Now that I've talked to Susan and the kids and to you, I feel like I'm more in control. More confident. I know you guys didn't have much of an opinion of me this last year. I had to play the game of the wishy-washy. It was the only way to cope with my predicament."

"Don't dwell on it," directed Randall. "You did the best you could. And believe me, you played the role well. It wasn't until we got Eastland's report that we began to suspect that something was going on."

"I appreciate that," said Martin sincerely.

"Don't think it's going to be easy," warned Randall. "There is eventually going to be a lot of bad publicity. You are going to have a hell of a re-election fight. But for what it's worth, Helen and I and a lot of other folks around here will back you up 100%. We don't give a damn what your sexual preferences are Bobby. You're still a hell of a good Senator. You've got a lot to offer. Not many people in your situation would have the guts to talk about it. People will respond to that, I think."

"Thanks Randall. You too, Helen. I appreciate your support. I don't deserve it but I sure appreciate it. I'll contact Park later today. I'll let you know how it goes."

"One more thing," Helen added. "I wouldn't talk to Wayne about anything."

Martin looked puzzled as he stopped at the door. "Do you suspect him?"

"Well let's just say he's been behaving strangely recently. I'd rather not take any chances."

He left awkwardly, not sure if he should say anything else, and perplexed at their final warning about his good friend Wayne Davis.

CHAPTER EIGHT

The flashbulbs and bright lights partly blinded Chairman Tanaka as he tried not to squint at the cameras. He was sitting in the Senate caucus room in front of the backdrop of the State Seal, a spot specially designed for such occasions.

"I have a brief statement to read and then I'll take a few questions," he stated, trying to sound like the state department spokesmen he admired on national television.

"The Joint House & Senate Special Committee on Pesticides and Contamination, having met on seven occasions and held exhaustive public hearings, has completed its final report. The majority concludes that there is no basis for public concern either over the safety of meat products or of drinking water in Hawaii."

Barbara Lum felt Tanaka's words were like a gauntlet thrown down to the press. If there was nothing to worry about, why so much energy and expense to investigate? Where there is smoke there is fire, she thought, enjoying the image of herself as tough and unyielding.

"We would at this time like to express our appreciation for the many citizens who shared their time and thoughts with us, as well as the dedicated public servants who came forward with their expertise. We realize that not everyone will be satisfied with our conclusions, but we must act responsibly in evaluating and separating the hearsay from the hard evidence. In fact, we have no scientifically substantiated evidence that our beef or our water are unsafe."

Tanaka glanced up and could see the faces of the media staring at him, some busy scribbling, other following the printed text. A few looked at him with aggression, others with disbelief. He had seen it before. He was a pro, and he was prepared for the barrage of questions to follow. As if to delay that inevitable moment, he paused deliberately between paragraphs. He methodical reading of the text, he hoped, might dull some of their eagerness.

"In reaching our conclusions, we have drawn upon the best scientific researchers available to us in our State. We have asked the hard questions. We have explored every possibility. There just is no basis for continued public concern."

"Senator Tanaka…Senator Tanaka, do you think…"

"Please Barbara, may I finish my statement?" Tanaka was the master of the first names of reporters to deflect the image of friction between the press and himself. The first name meant we are all part of the same team trying to do our job. There are no bad guys or good guys. We are all in it together. It made it harder for the viewing public to see him as an enemy.

"In the spirit of openness and democracy, we have included in the appendix a minority report signed by several members of the committee who reached other conclusions. We have no desire to suppress their viewpoints, although the majority has clearly rejected them."

"Finally, the majority wants to especially note at this time that the State Department of Health and Safety is officially absolved of any wrongdoing or negligence in this matter. They have acted professionally and in the best interests of the people of Hawaii. Questions?"

"Mr. Chairman," shouted several reports at once, each with the most important question that had to be asked.

"Fred?" Tanaka nodded to the older balding man who always wore a wrinkled jacket with his shirt partly hanging out of his pants.

"Mr. Chairman, why did your committee discount the testimony of Mrs. Flora Garcia, the woman who children got sick on the Smithville water?"

Tanaka looked at Fred, disappointed that his old friend would be so unkind. He had expected one of those leading questions that would have allowed Tanaka to expand on his role of leadership in the committee.

"We did not discount the testimony of any citizen. All viewpoints were taken into consideration. But just because someone, who incidentally is not trained in medicine, believes they were poisoned from a well does not mean that in fact they were. Indeed, we have included in Appendix II a letter, or rather a short report, from Paradise Underwriters indicating that the well in question was tested and found harmless. We appreciate the concern, but we decline to jump to conclusions."

"Senator, Todd Oshiro from the Herald? How did you feel taking over for Senator Bridges?"

"Mr. Oshiro, we were all deeply shocked and saddened by the Senator's untimely death. But the public's work must go on. We did the best we could to pick up the pieces. You must remember that no one person in our great system is indispensable." *And that SOB*, thought Tanaka, *was very dispensable.* His voice had a slight edge to it in his last statement. He recognized it himself, and at a cooler time might have controlled it. It was not good to be unkind to the dead. But in this case his enjoyment of his new role and the absence of an old rival gave him just a little too much pleasure to be resisted. He was watching Barbara Lum's face when he said it, and could see her wince, just barely.

"Mr. Chairman," Barbara snapped, "Yesterday Senator Tokugawa and others presented their minority report which completely contradicts your conclusions." Lum could see Tanaka straighten up, prepared for a defensive response. "How is it that the minority heard and read the same testimony and failed to reach the same conclusions?"

"I'm sorry Ms. Lum, but there is no accounting for taste." Tanaka led a chorus of hardy chuckles, but he did not notice his was considerably louder than the rest. He hoped that his flippant remark had removed the need to seriously answer the question.

Tanaka had done his best to avoid the embarrassment of a minority report. Other members of the committee, especially Michael Robinson, had been especially active. He had come up with the insurance report on the well, a late entry but welcome. Tanaka had wondered what Michael had said to Helen last week when he found her screaming at him in the hall way.

"You beast, Michael. Who the hell do you think you are, anyway? You think you can pressure me into keeping quiet?"

"Helen, look," Michael snidely retorted, "if you don't want it leaked out you know what you can do. Just stifle the minority report. Then your secret paper is safe."

"You swine. Never. Never!" She was next to tears now. Not just because of what Michael was trying to do, but because of who had betrayed her. Wayne Davis, her father figure in the Senate, had lied to Betsy to get the paper, and then, what really hurt, had given it to Michael, who threatened to give it to the Crusade Against Liberals. The CAL had fielded a candidate against Helen in the past as was known to be raising funds to target her in the next election. In recent years the CAL had become more influential since the editor of the Honolulu Herald had been 'born Again' and joined the CAL board of directors. She could see the headlines already: "LIBERAL POL PENS RED THESIS." It would be used to raise funds in the right wing community against her.

Michael's threat had not changed Helen's mind, for the minority report had come out just the same, perhaps with even more fanfare than it would have. Tanaka did not bother to ask Robinson what the argument was all about, and he was not sure he wanted to know.

Lum was not easily put off. She was ready for her big question. "Senator, how did the fact that a member of your committee, Representative Michael Robinson, is a member of the Board of Directors of the Palaka Produce Company affect your point of view?"

Somewhat uncertain, Tanaka answered "What are you getting at?"

"Representative Robinson is on the Palaka Board, which is a holding company for both the Sandwich Isle Chemical Corporation and the Smithville Plantation. Mrs. Garcia charged that the water from Smithville was toxic. My question, Senator, has to do with to what extent such a relationship may have influenced your deliberations. Isn't there a conflict of interest?"

"I would rather not speculate on the private business lives of the committee members," said Tanaka, somewhat taken aback by Lum's revelation. Even he had not been aware of Michael's arrangement. "I think we've covered all the main points. Thank you, one and all, for coming today. Mahalo."

Richard Tanaka quickly stood up to punctuate the end of the press conference, but there was really no need. Several reporters were trying to corner Barbara Lum to clarify what she had just said. Of course, professional competition would yield no more information, but quite a number of inquiries would be made in the next few days to the office of Michael Robinson, and to the corporate office of Palaka Produce.

Lum had taken a risk there. She had revealed to her competitors a major lead, which gave her an edge in the story. But she had to know whether or not Michael Robinson's conflict, if made public, would stimulate action, perhaps cause a mistake. She was not disappointed.

***

Stephen Sinclair leaned into his ten-speed and peddled up a steep hill about a mile from the old entrance to the Smithville Plantation. After finding Wilcox's fingerprints matching those on the glass and bottle in Bridges' office, and after hearing about Smithville from Helen, it was high time somebody actually tried to find out if chemicals were being dumped. He coasted down the next hill and tried to shift the weight of the cameras in his knap sack. Just down the road he could spot the small cluster of plantation camp houses where Flora lived.

He tried to peddle nonchalantly through the nearly abandoned village. A few young children, tanned and barefoot, stopped their play to notice him. Several older women were gathered in the tiny front yard of their friend to admire a Japanese type garden and to gossip. Every wooden house was a faded green with a hint of white trim. *It must have been thirty years since they were last painted*, Sinclair thought. He felt highly conspicuous, and surely would have been the subject of intense curiosity in a thriving community. But the few residents left in this camp lived in the past, or struggled with a dying lifestyle. They had no interest or time for the outsider today. The sun was hot and their flowers needed watering.

Sinclair coasted past the Garcia home, identified by a crooked nameplate on the mailbox. It was obviously abandoned. He could see through the open door that the furniture had been removed. An old calendar still hung in the shadows on a dingy wall. He wondered if she had moved her family as a result of the controversy over her testimony.

The dusty road ended abruptly at an abandoned field, once the edge of the plantation. Today it was mostly tall grass, bushes and weeds. He noticed a footpath that led into the underbrush. He could hear the trickle of a stream just beyond, barely audible above the quiet rustle of the grass and the buzzing insects in the hot sun. His skin already itched with the irritation of sweat and grime from the trip out. He could use a relaxing rest with his feet in a cool stream.

He parked his bike just out of sight and it took but two minutes to find the small brook. But it was hardly inviting. There was a kind of oily slick in the water - the rocks were without moss - the waters without any visible sign of stream life. As he peered closer at the streambed, he detected a faint odor, something chemical, unpleasant and irritating to the nose. He hadn't noticed it before because the breeze was blowing from the village out into the fields. His curiosity aroused, Sinclair decided to follow the stream bed upstream in the chance he might find the source of the pollution.

Sinclair hiked several hundred yards and just as he was passing a hill on his right he noticed that the stream had changed its character. Rather suddenly it had become healthy again. Somewhere in the last few hundred feet, he had missed something. He retraced his steps, this time inspecting the streambed carefully. Just about directly opposite the hill he noticed that the stream life seemed to fade and the slick appeared. But he could not identify the exact point where the change occurred. It was more of a gradual zone, as if the offending substance was oozing up from an unseen source.

It was just a whim that led him to hike to the top of the knoll. He was completely unprepared for what he saw. On the other side of the hill, partly concealed even from his position, was a depression in the terrain, the bottom of a distinct earthly bowl. Winding its way to the site was a dirt road, which Sinclair deduced ran out to the main highway. Where the road ended were several pieces of large machinery: a backhoe, a bulldozer, a forklift. There were several large piles of recently dumped dirt. Sinclair could not quite make out the bottom of the bowl so he hunched over and crept about ten yards to his left, stopping at a pile of rocks to remove his knapsack and take out his camera.

His new perspective told the story. Near the backhoe was a huge trench. At the bottom he could see several dozen large 50 gallon drums, which had been dumped and partly covered with dirt. About ten remained outside the trench. He quickly attached his 200 mm lens to get a better look at the labels: DANGER – TRIPTHANOL – DO NOT EXPOSE DIRECTLY TO SKIN, followed by a skull and crossbones – the universal symbol of poison. He began snapping pictures.

As he moved a little closer to get a better angle, a pickup truck roared into the clearing, with two workers riding in the back. They jumped out and slowly moved towards the idle machinery. Sinclair did not recognize any of them, except the driver of the truck, who seemed to be their supervisor. In the next few minutes, as Sinclair hid in the tall grass and collected his photographic evidence, a fork lift positioned the remaining drums next to the trench. The bulldozer then pushed the drums into the trench and began covering them with the remaining piles of dirt. Another vehicle arrived, a black limousine. The supervisor leaned over and appeared to be in consultation with a passenger in the back seat. The two laborers wore heavy boots and were raking dirt over the covered trench, obviously attempting to obscure any evidence of the buried barrels. Sinclair fumbled with his camera as he changed film.

He tried to keep an eye on the action as he re-wound the spool. A man got out of the limo and shouted directions to the crew. They stopped work and returned to the pick-up. Another man took the driver's seat, and the truck drove off down the narrow road, leaving a cloud of dust rising from the exit. The supervisor was in animated conversation with the back seat passenger.

Sinclair could not, on reflection, remember all the details of what happened next. If it had not been for the pictures he took he would still not believe it. A tall blond man in casual dress emerged from the driver's seat. He seemed to have something in his hand. The supervisor backed up towards the open trench.

The supervisor waved his hands…click…the blond man waved his object…click…there was a muffled spit…the supervisor fell backwards…click…only his feet protruded from the trench…click… the blond man stooped to push the body completely in…click…he walked to the bulldozer…click…he mounted…click, the machine began pushing dirt into the last few feet of the trench…click… the blond man dismounted…click…he slid into the limousine and quickly drove off…click…nothing left but dust again.

Sinclair clutched the camera as he hurried back along the path near the stream, feeling both excitement and fear. He prayed for his safety on the long ride home.

***

CHAPTER NINE

"*So-called Liberals like Senator Helen Tokugawa are strangling us with their schemes for more government control. A society must resist these well-meaning but misplaced efforts to extend the partisan machine every more into the future. It's time for a change in perspective,*" wrote the editor.

Randal Ogawa put down the newspaper he had been reading aloud. He looked at Helen, and tried to reflect in his face the same mixture of anger and political fear he saw in her eyes. They sat opposite each other in the reception area of Randall's second floor office. The secretary was on her lunch hour so they were alone.

"I guess it's already begun," she said. The last election had not been easy. It took several re-election efforts before an incumbent could be considered secure in his or her seat. She was still a relatively new star in the Senate. Newcomers were favorite temptations for ambitious opponents. She had expected to be 'targeted' for elimination. She had walked door-to-door in her entire Senate district two times to counteract the amount of money spent against he in the last election.

"Don't let them psych you out," advised Randall, reading her mind. "You know as well as anyone that this is the time to coolly set out a game plan. You be the one who controls the pace. You get a plan and you stick to it. Don't panic. Leave the panic to the other guys. You've done a good job. People know that. It should be easier raising money this time around."

"It better be. The Coalition Against Liberals is out for blood. They have turned the word *liberal* into an obscenity. They enclose it in quotations. They contort their faces when they say it. It's similar to the McCarthyism of the fifties."

"Aren't you exaggerating?"

"Maybe. But I have just been out in the district. You know, those town meetings I was talking to you about. People are more and more willing to accept broad labels. It's scary how susceptible perfectly intelligent people can be to this broad brush kind of stuff. I talked to a man who said he liked what I was doing, liked my independence. He also said he was telling all his friends to vote for the other party. 'We've got to get rid of the machine,' he said."

"He doesn't think of you as the machine, does he?"

"If he bothers to think carefully about me, no. But in a big election sometimes it's the gut that controls things. And now, with this manuscript thing, maybe I have just given the CAL nuts more ammunition."

"Yes, your paper." Randall was in a scolding mood. "You should know better than to give it to any politician, even Eastland.'

"I know, I know," she answered, somewhat sadly.

"Actually, don't misunderstand me. I liked it. I thought it was a provocative piece. After all, how many people active in politics think deeply about ideas and to write them down? Yeah, you were young. Yeah, you were inexperienced. But it wasn't half bad. The stupid thing was letting it get around."

"It's not because politicians can't write," Helen countered, "it's just because they're too smart. They know it's dangerous. They are not lacking in words or thought. In most ways they are a lot brighter than you or I. So let's not get hung up on how neat it is to have written something. We need a clear headed assessment here, Senator!"

"Right. As I was saying. I think it was courageous to link the ethnic struggle and the class struggle directly. And recently, you know we both agree that the Party has been coasting on ethnicity for too long. It's time for ideas, and especially time to get off this circle-the-wagons bit."

Helen chuckled to herself. "The other day someone pointed out that it's OK to circle the wagons but sooner or later everyone has to take a you-know-what, and that leaves everyone standing in their own you-know-what..." She and Randall shared a genuine laugh. "But this is all irrelevant, as I used to say all the time. Even if my old paper presents some food for thought, it won't be cooked well."

"It could fill a big vacuum. Nobody seems to be discussing openly the meaning of various philosophies these days."

"At least your paper didn't go after the media."

"True, but if I were to rewrite it, I would. In the last few months, it has really come to me. You know that popular talk show on radio? I've listened a dozens times and not once has that guy said anything positive about government."

"Well, that's his role. That's what media people feel they must do, act as a balance of sorts." Randall was only half sincere as he egged her on.

"I have no problem with that. But today people are so cynical and demoralized about their government. When they hear, day after day, about how elected or appointed officials are just a bunch of turkeys, or lazy, or whatever, they begin to lose faith." Helen was getting angrier the more she thought of it.

"Come on, Senator, aren't you being a little over sensitive?"

"You bet I'm sensitive. I'm sensitive about democracy and its reputation. People think there are major alternatives to the democratic process. That a legislature, which is a bundle of appetites and interests, should behave as efficiently as a single dictator. Well, it's a sloppy process. Society is complex. We reflect that complexity. When the media tries to tell people that society is simple, that the solutions are simple, then that is what I call a disservice."

"Listen to yourself," Randall cautioned. "You sound like an apologist for the system. I thought you were frustrated, anxious for reform. Tired of the old cronies. A closet revolutionary."

"It depends on what you want to revolutionize, Randall, you know that. Sure the system needs more energy, more of a sense of urgency, and heaven knows more of a sense of excellence. But that doesn't mean we should teach everyone to hate the system. There is only one alternative when you get to that point."

"What is that, professor?"

"Don't patronize me! I don't need your glibness; I need your support!" Helen was a little shocked at how harsh her words were. Randall was hurt that she felt he was not taking her seriously. If anything, he always took her seriously.

After a short pause while she searched the Punchbowl skyline visible from his window, Helen turned to make her point. "The alternative the media wants is to listen to the media, to regard them as the single voice of authority. And the problem with that is that there is too much competition for attention to inhibit the irresponsible. It's too easy to become sensational at the expense of the facts, just to get listeners or readers, just to attract more advertising money."

"Ah, the Marxist returns to the Senate. No, don't take me wrong. I just get amused to think what the Coalition Against Liberals would do with a tape of what you just said. They probably would accuse you of Satanism or something. Communism, at least."

"Based on who they include in that category I'd say I was in pretty good company. Most of the known world," she said, easing off from her near tantrum.

Helen closed her eyes then said reflectively, "I can't believe what Wayne did, after we included him in everything, after we trusted him. I wonder just how involved he might be with Michael." It was obviously one more complication they did not need.

"You said Sinclair called a little while ago?" Randall thought it best to change the subject. He would figure out a way to handle Wayne.

"I've never heard him so agitated. He insisted we meet immediately! He should be here in a few minutes. Something about his excursion out to the old Smithville property."

Neither Helen nor Randall expected to see what Stephen Sinclair showed them that evening. The pictures were developed immediately after his trip to the plantation. "This is no longer a matter of civil corruption or environmental cover-up. We're talking heinous criminal acts here. We've got to go to the police right now. It may even be necessary for your own personal safety. These guys are playing for keeps."

***

The KARE ten o'clock news increased their sense of urgency. Barbara Lum had wasted no time in following up on Sinclair's initial leads.

"It has been learned by KARE NEWS that a prominent state legislator may be financially involved in a major conflict of interest concerning the contamination of wells. Representative Michael Robinson is listed as a member of the board of directors of Palaka Produce. This holding company actually owns both the old Smithville Plantation, where Mrs. Flora Garcia claims to have had her water contaminated, and the Sandwich Island Chemical Corporation, which at one time supplied pesticides to Smithville.

"A spokesman for Sandwich Isle told this reporter that the ownership of his company by Palaka was only for tax purposes and in no way affected policy decisions. When asked if he knew who was on the board of Palaka, he said he had not seen a list of the directors for some time."

"Representative Robinson could not be reached for comment on whether his interests in Palaka and Smithville had any bearing on his decision to sign the Majority Report of the Joint Subcommittee which investigated charges of pollution. The Majority Report found no evidence of a public health hazard. A Minority Report filed by several Senators led by Helen Tokugawa disagreed strongly with the majority position."

"In a related story, KARE sources in New York have learned that large amounts of Palaka Produce stock are being purchased on behalf of insurance interests in London. Palaka Produce Executive Director Sam Butler confirmed this report, but declined to comment on how it could affect the company. Reporting live from the State Capitol, this is Barbara Lum for KARE NEWS."

This news report did not go unnoticed by Ramsey Bingham, as he looked up from his favorite paper, the *Pacific Business Daily*. He reached for the phone and asked for the Kahala Hilton Hotel. "Mr. Carleton Brent, please."

***

"I was an only child, and I think I turned out OK," said Helen, raising an eyebrow in mock seriousness. She sipped a little more white wine and leaned just slightly against Randy. They were sitting side by side on Helen's small couch with their shoes off and feet propped up on one of the office chairs.

"Large families can be a real drain," said Randy, enjoying the feeling of Helen's head against his shoulder. "I can remember the fights over hand-me-downs, and a very painful decision as to who would go to college."

"I have the feeling that sending kids to college is going to be harder. The cost of even most public schools is going through the roof," said Helen, finding this preliminary rehearsal of domesticity enjoyable. Her adult life had been preoccupied with ideas, issues, and politics. She had never had the interest or the time for other more personal concerns. But the last two years had mellowed her, and the man she sat next to this evening was becoming more than just a professional colleague.

"They probably will have to work during high school," Randy offered, pushing the limits of their tacit understanding.

"It's bad enough raising one child, and two would just about be it. A friend of mine is what I'd consider a model parent, and his son was just arrested for selling drugs. Sometimes I think that you have to be the opposite of what you want your kids to be, just so they can rebel in the right direction," said Helen, allowing herself to wander into a future she seldom contemplated.

"Working is important, although you don't want to cut off opportunities for self improvement," Randy continued. They were both aware that he had spent many an hour building his confidence while earning a black belt in Karate. He was not tall, but his body was well developed and contained a quiet assurance common to those who excelled in martial arts and also understood their philosophy. This combination of humility and confidence was one of the things that had attracted Helen to Randy in the first place. So many of the men she knew in politics tried to exaggerate their importance in small but comic physical habits. They swaggered, they strutted, and they tried to overcome their insecurities with outward bravado. It was not blatant, just subtle little quirks that Helen had trained herself to notice. Randy was different. He put his weaknesses forward, and concealed his strengths. And as a result, nearly everyone liked him. Most knew about his personal struggle to overcome poverty, the early death of his father, and how he had worked to put his younger brother and sister through high school and college.

"As long as both of us, I mean, as long as both parents work, it should not be too difficult raising a couple of kids, or at least paying for them," said Helen as she blushed to think how dangerously direct their remarks were getting.

Randy quickly finished his wine and got up from the couch, somewhat embarrassed, and somewhat pleased. They had formally begun their courtship, and while neither had made an overt commitment, both were warmed by the belief that they had found that special person.

"We'd better get going, it's after midnight and I've got an early morning breakfast," Randy said, providing the excuse to conclude their quiet time together.

"And I've got some correspondence to write. Mind putting the wine back in the ice box?" They had hardly had anything to drink, but somehow they had not needed it.

The capitol was dark as they left the office. Occasionally you could see one of the security guards patrolling the outer hallways. Nevertheless, Helen was glad not to be alone. She remembered several years ago a woman had been attacked in the stairwell. Her thoughts of danger were quickly forgotten as she walked closely to Randy, happy to just be with him.

They descended the private elevator for Senators, and walked through the dim narrow halls in the basement leading to the parking area. Their thoughts were on each other and the meaning of their talk. As they exited out into the cement garage Randall barely noticed the shift in the shadows behind a large van. It was only a reflex habit that made him lightly turn his head away from Helen and towards the movement.

Helen, reflecting several hours later on what happened, could not remember seeing or hearing anything until suddenly Randall was struck with a knife by a lunging assailant. Randall had apparently deflected the blow, and recovered enough to pull the attacker down onto the cement floor. She had found herself screaming, shrieking in a way that she had not thought herself capable. She saw arms and legs striking at each other. Randall's karate was barely a match for the larger man. He must have been nearly seven feet tall. She could see the knife flash as they struggled. She was paralyzed with fear for Randy.

Randall had been able to parry the first thrust, although not without sustaining a minor wound to his shoulder and neck. He felt no pain as his entire body was alerted, instantly hyped on its own adrenalin. His foot rose smoothly and planted itself in the large man's groin, yet that seemed only to slow him down. It gave Ogawa just enough time to pull him down to the floor again, in the hope of gaining some leverage or advantage. They tumbled, Ogawa's iron grip on the man's knife-wielding arm weakened by another wound, somewhere. A blow to the assailant's throat was off center, but caused him to pause. Ogawa was able to stand up, crouching for the next engagement. The man lunged and Ogawa gambled by moving to meet the deadly hand and cripple its force. His foot was not set to handle the force of their collision. The knife hand broke away from Ogawa's grip and plunged itself into his side.

For one eternal moment Helen stared into the face of the blue-eyed attacker, who knelt next to Randall's bleeding form. The man's eyes shifted as he caught sight of the security guard rounding the corner. He lurched towards the exit on the far side of the parking garage. The guard pulled his gun and fired in his direction. The man wrenched the heavy door open and escaped up the stairs into the dark night air. Randall Ogawa lay wounded at Helen's feet, his blood staining the bottoms of her high heeled shoes.

CHAPTER TEN

Helen tried not to let on to anyone she met the next day just how really shaken she was. She postponed her meeting with Meiling and tried to clear her head as she drove to the police station for her second meeting with Byron Park. She hadn't slept much, in shock over the brutal episode in the parking garage, endless questions by the police, then waiting for word about Randy at the hospital. Thank goodness he would be alright, she thought, praying that the doctor's immediate assessment of his wounds was accurate.

Byron Park was in a serious mood when he ordered Helen and Stephen Sinclair into the small wood-paneled conference room. It was built in the thirties, and the varnish had been worn off the table and chairs. The glass partitions of the upper walls let in light through a clouded and stained filter. The walls were yellow, and the room smelled of cigarettes.

"I'll spare you the lecture on why you should not be trying to do my job. Needless to say, if you had been a little more forthcoming, one death and one assault might have been avoided," he began. "There is an all points bulletin out with the description you gave us on the assailant, Senator. And you, Mr. Private Investigator, you could be in a lot of trouble. However, I must admit that those pictures you brought in are incredible. We have sent a team out to the site. Incidentally, Senator, you should take a closer look at the killer in Sinclair's pictures. He could be the same man who attacked you and Senator Ogawa last night. As for the fingerprints, let's just say I forgot to ask how you obtained them."

Even Park was surprised about the prints, and embarrassed. Sinclair had found what the department should have found in the first place, if they had done their job properly. He left the room several times and returned with forms for them to fill out. He had another detective join them for a discussion on fingerprints. He made a call to the prosecutor.

It took over three hours of this 'administrivia,' as Helen called it, before she suspected that Park was constructing a plan of action. She had fantasized that along with Randall and Mei-ling they could have "brought the swine to justice," as Randall said. But now she realized how far in over their heads they had been.

Park interrogated Helen extensively on the relationship of Bobby Martin to Eastland, and made passing mention that Martin had been to see him. It was clear that for the first time Byron Park was completely in charge of whatever was going to happen next.

These politicians, he thought. *They seem to make a career out of getting involved in things they know nothing about.* Park was not really cynical, just indifferent, convinced that it was the administrative department, the "guys on the line," as he put it, who got things done. Politics was beyond his interests or understanding.

These cops, Helen thought. *They think just because they have the criminal justice system behind them, and all those resources, that they are the only ones who can figure anything out. They think society is their territory, period.* Helen was not really anti-police, just a little resentful that she was on their turf. It was easy to imagine, as a legislator, that everything, virtually everything, was one's turf. That fantasy ended when confronted with the real world on the streets.

"Alright," Park announced as he charged back into the conference room after leaving Sinclair and Helen to cool their heels for at least 45 minutes. "I want you two here tomorrow morning at ten sharp, got it?" It was more of a command than a question. His listeners nodded. "And between now and then I don't want a word about this to anyone. That includes Senator Ogawa, Senator," Park said to Helen. "I understand that he will be making a full recovery in time, and I have no doubt that sooner or later someone from the press is going to talk to him. I need your help in delaying that event as long as possible. Perhaps the doctors can help us out, say he needs more rest. And you need to find a way to refuse any statements to them. Anyway, we are going to need your cooperation in catching those responsible, and I'd like to keep the knowledge of what we do secure."

"No arguments here, Detective, "said Helen. Sinclair nodded in agreement when Park look at him for confirmation. After they had left, Park went back to his private office at the far end of the hall. "They're gone now. You can leave in about ten minutes," he said politely to Bobby Martin. Martin wondered why the secrecy. He knew that they all were on the same side. Park offered no explanation. He sat down at his desk and began writing. Park looked up again, dismissing him with his eyes."

"So, ten o'clock, and I know, don't talk to anyone," said Martin. Park continued to stare at him. With some discomfort and awkwardness, Martin nodded and left.

Detective Byron Park had learned over the years that often the best way to investigate was to be invisible and let people make their mistakes. He had applied this principle to the Bridges case, and it had finally paid off. There was something about this so-called accidental death that did not feel right. He sensed it with Helen Tokugawa and Bobby Martin back in the initial stages of the investigation. He sensed that Mei-ling Bridges had been trying to tell him something, too. But for some reason, the fact that Bridges was in politics complicated everything. It wasn't just another dead man. There was more at stake. People tended to hide things when more was at stake. People also tended to up the ante. In the end, the stakes would get too high for somebody. It was also his belief that when you moved in to set the trap it was best to keep as many people ignorant as possible. *Knowledge created stress, and stress changed behavior. Once people started acting differently, the guilty become wary.*

The file on the Bridges case was now several inches thick. Park fingered its contents for clues or reminders of pieces to the puzzle. His notes on the initial interviews…photocopies of the organizational papers and Directors of Palaka Produce, the Sandwich Isle Chemical Corporation…employees of the Smithville operation…and a copy of a letter given to him by Betsy Ito on the advice of Helen.

Perhaps Park had been a bit harsh on Tokugawa. After all, she had sent Betsy his way. She had arranged for some of the initial interviews. And she had sent Bobby to him, the major break in the case, at least before last night. Nevertheless, he had wanted to impress upon her who was in charge.

He skimmed once again the newspaper stories of the legislative hearings, which were paper clipped to an affidavit signed by Flora

Garcia. It was filed as a result of his visit to her house, when she showed him the stream and its odor. But Park was not in the business of protecting the environment, his business was protecting witnesses. It was on his recommendation that the Garcia family was provided with housing far away from Smithville.

Park glanced at his watch. It was time to meet the rest of the team and search for the body Sinclair saw buried. He did not relish the prospect of a corpse submerged in a toxic chemical called trip to-something or other.

Let's go Byron," came a muffled voice from the door. Park looked up and saw his visitor dressed head to toe in a silver space suit, with a gas mask under his arm. Park walked warily behind the Department of Health & Safety inspector out to the truck where people form the coroner's office were waiting, wondering what kind of chemical this might be.

***

"Look Brent, I know this industry. So far, I can say for sure that we are the only ones who present this kind of a...problem. We made some unwise investments, we overcapitalized, and we joined the Sandwich Isle Group with the plantation. If you help us to get out from under it clean, we can continue to do business for many years." Ramsey Bingham searched the arrogant face of his English associate, unable to detect what effect his words were having. Bingham had spent a lifetime learning to read faces, and in the islands there was none better. But this man was foreign, in his thinking, and in his reactions.

"Bingham, admit it, you're just a renegade. All the other people in agriculture in Hawaii have played by the rules. You didn't. You tried to bend them to your liking. The other agribusiness accounts we have are all investing in bio-technology. They're splicing genes, developing new pest resistant strains. Personally, my view is that Ag will die before they make the big breakthroughs, but they are trying. They are even leading the way in research to control the spread of pesticides. But not you, not the great Ramsey Bingham. You are still making money on chemical fertilizers."

"That money pays handsome premiums to our insurance Agency," retorted Bingham, disliking Brent more by the minute.

"Yes, you have been profitable. Especially your overseas contracts. Thank God the third world hasn't any of these environmentalists. You can spread those toxins as thick as you want and nobody is going to complain. Your lucrative profits were what led us to increase our investments in Palaka Produce."

"You were just hedging your bets, Brent." Brent smiled, glad that the preliminary sparing was coming to an end. There was nothing as tiresome as having to pretend one was trying to help a man you were trying to use.

"Don't worry, our inclination is not to pull out of agriculture, not yet anyway. But the Sandwich Island Chemical Corporation has become an embarrassment. We do not like such embarrassments. And you have been unable to keep it in-house. "We have to"- he paused, searched for the correct words that suggested just enough but which could never mean anything in a court of law "- assign additional personnel to this case. This costs us more to maintain our investments, not to mention ensure a substantial risk Against liability. My trip alone should not have been necessary."

Bingham did not bother to point out that the trip was more a vacation than a necessity. Still, he was deeply troubled by the recent turn of events, and the loss of control over the entire operation. Ramsey Bingham was easily capable of blackmail, but beyond that…"

'So what about our policy, are you going to cancel?

"We have looked very carefully, and for the time being are willing to continue coverage. We appreciate the American laws which require all chemical operations and agricultural interests to be insured. We feel it is not in our interest to force you into bankruptcy, not just yet. But you must be aware that the liabilities have increased geometrically. Through your clumsiness, you have got a whole herd of publicity hungry politicians sniffing about. This is why we took the action which was necessary. And there may be more we will require to assure our investors of a sound return." Bingham did not like the sounds of this last prediction, but he was smart enough to know it was not a good idea for him to know about it.

"But you intend to raise our rates. So how much?"

"We intend to raise your rates, yes. We have examined your books and feel you can easily absorb a 300% increase. It is just based on your risk, Mr. Bingham. Surely you understand. Business is business."

Bingham left the Kahala Hilton consciously trying to control his temper, barely avoiding a car accident as he drove back to town. He had built an effective empire in Hawaii, and now this snotty Englishman was telling him how to run his business. He could feel the sense of panic rising slowly these last few weeks. He could feel the sense of isolation. Yesterday, Clarence Soong of the very same industry he had built told him over the phone the other owners wanted no part of any cover-up. They were even willing to accept more controls over the use of pesticides. They did not need the aggravation, nor the additional loss of public support for agriculture.

Bingham drove along the idyllic tree-lined Kahala Avenue, home of the stars, location of TV and movie filming. He had once aspired to live on this street, with a private tennis court, his backyard looking out on the beach, his only civic gripe the inconvenience of getting in and out on Honolulu Marathon Sunday in December, when ten thousand health nuts slogged up and down this very road. *We still might make it, a neighbor of the elite.* But that would never happen if he didn't find a way to put a lid on the Garcia case. Now, enter Brent and his henchman, what was his name? Niles? It was his Kahala dream that had stiffened his resolve and allowed Nils to execute his foreman, Bill Wilcox. I never imagined it would come to this, he thought, hoping his shock was an adequate substitute for genuine remorse, if someone up there was watching. Ramsey Bingham might have been unscrupulous, but never a criminal. Not until lately.

As he drove up the short hill past the Triangle Park and on up around Diamond Head, Bingham tried to distract himself by analyzing what he knew about Brent. *Could he bring Brent down, if need be? He wasn't going to take the blame for him. What am I saying? Take the blame. This can still be handled. We can still come out on top.*

By the time Bingham had descended Diamond Head and was driving on Ala Wai Boulevard he had been able to boost his own confidence. It was exactly this act of self delusion and resistance that Byron Park was counting on.

***

"His name is Carleton Brent. He's in town with his secretary and staying at the Kahala Hilton. The president of Paradise Underwriters had a special top secret meeting with him this morning," Bobby Martin explained, hoping that this information would be of help to Helen. "His secretary's name is Stephani, and according to our secretary, she's just one of those sexpots executives drag along with them for fun. Brent has been to Honolulu several times in the last ten years. He always brings some new woman with him. While Brent is holding discrete meetings at his hotel, Stephani has been shopping in Waikiki. That's about all I can find out, sorry."

"Thanks Bobby, I really appreciate it, I really do. Just one more favor through."

"What's that?"

"Don't tell anyone about what you found out, OK?" Martin agreed, wondering why everyone kept telling him not to talk to others. Byron Park had been almost obnoxious about it.

Helen felt like a caged animal. She was distraught over Randy's serious injuries, and determined to do something about it. She was cooperating as fully as possible with Park, but he basically was trying to keep her out of the way. She knew instinctively that there must be some outside force which stimulated the attack. Someone was in big trouble. Perhaps it was Bingham himself, but she suspected it was larger than that. When Martin called confirming her suspicions, she did not take long to concoct an ad-hoc plan. As much as she knew it was dangerous, she just could not sit still.

Mei-ling had been helpful. Together they talked about what a woman like Stephani might be like, what she would want, and how she might react. Mei-ling was insistent that Stephani could not be the mindless sex-machine that Brent hired her for. "She's using him," Mei-ling said. "She's after a better life, and the only way she knows how to get it is to toady to this man. But you can believe that deep down inside she resents him and what she must do." It was always fascinating to Helen how refined and almost pure Mei-ling was, and at the same time there was this other side to her. She understood the dark side of life, the inner appetites of men and women. She never let herself be less than a perfectly gracious lady amid the hard-boiled self interests of politics. *That's why she was such an asset to Eastland,* Helen reflected.

It was Mei-ling's idea for the meeting with Stephani. Helen was aware that this was her way of participating in the investigation. Mei-ling has been on the outside looking in, passively, for too long. She had to do something, and Helen provided her with an outlet.

"She should be approached while she is shopping, I think," Mei-ling continued. "You should call her by name, and say something that she cannot ignore, something that she must know more about. Once her interest is aroused, you can suggest coffee. The meeting should not be too long, because you will be nervous, and you don't want to make a mistake. The less opportunity she has to question you the better." Helen was amazed at how confident Meil-ling was about how people would behave. Just as Helen was a student of appearances and fine detail, Mei-ling was a master of the inner life. They agreed on Helen's wardrobe for the masquerade, and discussed in detail the kind of personality she should project.

****

Stephani was single-minded as she searched through the dress rack, quickly dismissing most, stopping to inspect one or two which caught her eye. She did this with a self assurance and confidence that Helen had often observed of women when shopping. It was not difficult to maneuver herself next to Stephani on the same rack, also intent on ferreting out that one dress she'd been looking for. Without turning her head, Helen said, "you're Stephani Harrison, aren't' you?" Stephani suspended her search and looked at Helen with astonishment.

"You know me?"

"I know you. You're travelling with Carleton Brent, aren't you?"

"I'm afraid I'm at a disadvantage here. Do I know you?"

Helen turned directly toward Stephani to emphasize the importance of what she was about to say.

"I used to be a…friend of Brent's. Just like you are his friend," said Helen, searching Stephani's eyes for recognition of her not-so-hidden meaning. "My name is Julia. I want to talk with you, perhaps over coffee," Helen gestured toward the coffee shop just beyond the dress racks.

"May I ask what you want with me?" answered Stephani as her eyes moved over Helen, looking for clues to who this woman was.

"It has to do with your relationship with Brent, and your future. I can tell you things you might find very, very interesting." Helen turned and began walking towards the coffee shop, confident that Stephani would follow. She was not disappointed.

Stephani's curiosity was aroused by this unexplainable encounter. But it was not so much the behavior or the words of Helen which caused her to follow. It was more her personal dissatisfaction with Brent that led her to believe that somehow this Julia represented a threat. She knew that Brent was a womanizer, although he claimed he was loyal to her. *Was she one of his former conquests? Was she a threat? Maybe she knows something about Brent that might be useful. Information is always useful.* She watched Helen from behind, noting her expensive punk outfit, and the heavy jewelry which seemed to advertise that this woman had been around and knew how to get what she wanted.

"He always used to take me to the Kahala Hilton, too," began Helen. Stephani tried not to show her displeasure at this revelation. "He always stayed a few days and then we were off to Maui. When he tired of me, this was about four years ago, it was without warning. He just checked out and left a crummy note about having a good life. It took me a long time to get over it, how he used me."

"So, Julia, what do you want from me?" Stephani was going to play the confident and secure one, trying not to show her own fears about what Brent might do with her

"Last night, your wonderful Mr. Brent called me up. He insisted we meet at another hotel, just for old time's sake, he said. I asked him if he was alone."

Stephani leaned slightly forward. This was obviously something she did not want to hear, but something she must know.

"He said, Ms. Harrison, that, and I quote, 'Nobody that is going to be around for long. Just a passing fling I've grown tired of. In fact, Julie baby, I'll be off to Maui alone, that is, unless if you'd care to join me.' Those were his exact words."

Stephani was grasping for a way to react which did not expose her distress. She added more sugar to her cup, which Helen noticed must be half full of sugar by now. She pretended it was just right, and reached to butter her croissant, her hand shaking just noticeably.

"Look Stephani, may I call you Stephani?" Helen asked, not waiting for an answer. "I'm one of those women Brent has used and abused. His overture last night was just like him, expecting forgiveness. He's a spoiled SOB who uses women, just like he's using you. How long do you think he's going to keep you around before he moves on to greener pastures?"

"What do you want?" snapped Stephani.

"I want revenge. I want to set this guy up and blackmail his ass, scuse the language. I want to make him think twice the next time he tries to purchase a person for his personal pleasure. And Ms. Harrison, I think that deep down inside you want the same thing."

There was a long silence as the waitress brought their salads. Finally, Stephani looked directly at Helen, this time with openness and honestly.

"You seem to know a lot about Brent, and about me. And you are not wrong, Julia, or whatever you name is. It's true, I'm not especially overjoyed with Brent, in fact, I'm sick of him. He is what I think you Americans might call a slime-bag." Helen had to hold back her laughter to maintain the intensity of the moment.

"You're interested in revenge, too?"

"Yes, I suppose I am. At least I'm interested in what you propose."

Helen outlined her scheme. Stephani understood that Brent's reputation depended on the utmost discretion. So did his business. People like Brent were almost compulsive about the privacy of their meetings. If Helen could produce pictures of Brent meeting with clients in Honolulu, he just might be willing to pay to get the negatives.

"So, what did you tell him when he called?" asked Stephani, trying to understand what Brent's frame of mind might be.

"I told him to go soak it, and that the next time he heard from me it would be on my terms, not his."

"So he knows you are upset."

"You bet he does. If you can find out his schedule, and I can get pictures of his meetings, we can make him believe that an old female acquaintance wants revenge, and money. He'll never suspect that you are in on it. All you have to do is tell him you were accosted by this crazy woman and given the photographs. If he doesn't want them circulated in Honolulu, and elsewhere, then he'd better come up with some cash. I've done some digging. I know that Brent is involved with a very controversial issue in Hawaii."

"What's that?"

"It has something to do with chemical pollution and several very prominent corporations and politicians. Brent is in insurance, right? So he's probably helping these people to avoid exposure. He certainly wouldn't want to be publically associated with them. Especially if they have something to hide."

"I see," said Stephani, not really understanding, but fully aware that public disclosure would be just the kind of thing Brent might pay to avoid."

"What's in it for me?" she asked, almost enjoying the prospect of getting something out of Brent, or at least seeing him squirm.

"Two things, which we share I think. We can get him to pay money. I'd say at least $100, 00 should be possible on short notice. We split the money. I'm in debt, and if he does plan to can you, you will at least have something to get you started. And, perhaps more important, the pleasure of squeezing HIM for a change. Letting him know that his past will catch up with him. Maybe he'll treat people a little differently in the future." Helen was hoping that Mei-ling was right about Brent's character, and Stephani's willingness to get even.

"So, let me get this straight. I get you his schedule. You take pictures. You give me the pictures, and I go to Brent. I tell him I met this woman and she wants money. I show him the pictures. Tell him instructions will arrive soon. I don't know anything about all this, so I pretend, but I am upset about this woman. I fuss a little about being jealous. He, you think, will deny any knowledge of you, certainly not let on about calling you. But he will admit that maybe in his past there was someone he forgot. He might agree to pay you the money. You contact him and arrange for a meeting place. He shows up with the cash. You give me half. And he never knows I was involved, right?"

"That's about it. I think we can pull it off, Stephani. I think we can both get what we want out of this. How about it? Are you game?"

After the meeting, Helen quickly drove home, hoping no one would recognize her, especially with the wig with orange streaks. She had forgotten how attuned she was to always being on public display, always ready to be watched. Even minor public figures unconsciously tidied up their wardrobes when they went out. *If someone actually recognized me in the get-up...*

She thought about how the meeting had gone with Stephani. Even though Brent had never heard of this Julia, and of course had never called her, she felt she had sold Stephani on the idea of the evening proposition by Brent, and more importantly, on his probable denial. That covered all her bases. Now all she had to do was wait for Stephani's call regarding Brent's schedule, and hope that Sinclair was creative enough to get pictures, and a small tape recorder.

CHAPTER ELEVEN

Stephen Sinclair lay on his back in the small rented row boat as it bobbed gently in the protected lagoon off the Kahala Hotel. His camera gear was well concealed on the floor of the boat, and he wondered if he would actually be able to get decent pictures from an unstable platform. His prey was sitting about a hundred yards away on a patio with three other men. As inconspicuously as possible he snapped off a series of shots with his long range lens. It would never do. He'd have to get closer.

The patio was surrounded by plants, had several round tables with beach umbrellas, and was connected to an inside lagoon where two friendly dolphins performed for hotel guests. It was not difficult for anyone using the adjacent beach to wander about the area, watching the dolphins, or the tourists.

Sinclair, now equipped with his more discrete smaller camera, strolled about the lounge area, snapping this and that, careful to include the four men talking amiably in the corner. He circled the area to ensure that all present would be clearly identifiable. The only one he could not be sure of was the rather tall fellow facing away from the ocean, towards the plants. He had to get him to turn around. A child's rubber beach ball rolling unattended was perfectly kicked to hit the man on the shoulder. He turned to see where it came from.

Click. A perfect shot. All five faces looking directly at the camera: Carleton Brent, Ramsey Bingham, Wayne Davis, and a very tall muscular man with blond hair. Sinclair was able to hide behind a group of tourists and was sure they suspected nothing. He hurried away, somewhat shaken by the presence of the man he had seen at the dump with the gun.

*****

"Police declined to comment on the source which led them to the site where a body was found in a shallow grave on the old Smithville Plantation," began

Barbara Lum. It was another in a series of reports she had been doing on the pesticide case, dubbed "Pestigate" by those convinced it would lead to a major scandal with political repercussions.

"William Wilcox, an employee of the Palaka Produce Company, was thought to be in his mid forties when he was apparently murdered sometime last week. His body was thrown into a ditch on top of several fifty gallon drums of toxic chemicals. The Coroner's Office issued a report stating that the cause of death was two bullet wounds in the chest. The police are looking for a tall man with blond hair for questioning. The State Department of Health and Safety said that they were investigating the burial of the drums and are looking to whether or not laws had been violated. Reporting live from the Smithville Plantation for KARE NEWS, this is Barbar Lum.

Helen reached over and pushed the remote control button to shut off the television. It was not a good idea for Randy to get upset, she reasoned. His eyes fell on hers and blinked in gratitude, then closed as he sought more rest. Helen could hardly control her emotions when she first saw him lying there, his chest all bandaged, and tubes in his mouth and nose. He could not communicate, but she knew that he appreciated her presence. She would sit with him and talk until he seemed too tired to listen. She told him what was happening in the case, but not her scheme to trap Brent and record incriminating evidence. The last thing she wanted for Randy to have to worry about her. It seemed that her life was now filled with people to care for. Not only Randy, but people like Betsy, who suffered both betrayal and then the loss of someone she cared for deeply.

"You know how men try to be macho with each other,' Helen had said. "He probably was just trying to sound, you know. The fact that they went after him that could indicate that he was caught in the middle. Maybe he really didn't betray you," she continued, hoping that Betsy would find it in her to forgive. Forgiving would make the healing more complete.

"If only I could be sure about Bill, about how he felt," Betsy had sobbed. Helen reached in her purse and pulled out a crumpled note. It was the one sent to Bobby Martin, the one intended for Betsy.

"Betsy, listen. There's something you must know. Bill Wilcox was involved in a scheme to blackmail Bobby. We have the evidence. Bobby has the evidence. But we think that Bill was just a pawn in a larger game. I want to show you something. Here."

Betsy read the note. She reached for Helen and sobbed as she hugged Helen for support. It was a painful time for both of them, and one reason why Helen had been anxious to get involved with the plot to entrap the man from London.

***

Helen was shaken when she saw the photos taken by Sinclair. There was Wayne Davis, sitting in conspiracy with Ramsey Bingham and that Carleton Brent. That was bad enough. But looking right into the camera lens was that other face, the one that had looked at her after knifing Randall in the basement parking garage. The man who had nearly killed Randy, was still on the loose.

She could imagine what Byron Park would say when he saw the photos. She had sent Sinclair directly to the police station, knowing that they would want to get to the Kahala Hilton before Brent and his henchman disappeared. Meanwhile, Helen waited patiently on the park bench facing the Waikiki Bandstand.

It was nearly dusk, just light enough to recognize someone and just dark enough to make a meeting unnoticed. According to Stephani, Brent seemed to have fallen for their trap perfectly. She had given him the packet of pictures, especially the ones taken by the pool. Helen was grateful that Stephani had not pressed to explain the other photo, the one showing Brent's Scandinavian associate talking to another man in an abandoned cane field. Helen knew that Brent could never allow such a photo to be circulated. It was even more of a concern than the pool-side meeting, although Stephani did not know that.

Helen's demand for a meeting was a gamble. She had no guarantee that Brent would react positively and actually bring money to pay off a long forgotten scorned woman. Stephani had not called back to report on Brent's plans. She probably was the last person he would tell. Perhaps he even threatened her, Helen suspected. Wouldn't it be hysterical if he actually showed up with the money? If should could only get him on tape, he would surely incriminate himself.

Helen's daydreams prevented her from noticing a man watching her from the street. He quietly moved in among the tall ironwood trees. The long drooping branches easily concealed him. There he waited until the early evening removed the remaining light from Kapiolani Park.

When Byron Park saw the photos delivered by Stephen Sinclair, he forced him to reveal Helen's plans. Sinclair told him part of it, but claimed ignorance about the site of any meeting. He was telling the truth. Only Mei-ling Bridges knew the full details of Helen's planned rendezvous.

***

Against his better judgment, Ramsey Bingham decided to take the call from Senator Bobby Martin personally. Bingham had meticulously avoided direct contact. It was his first rule of business: always insulate yourself from unpleasant decisions. But now there was no one else who could deal with Martin.

"Hello Senator, long time no see, so to speak. What can I do for you?"

There was a long pause, as Martin sought to communicate an iciness he felt was required for the proper effect.

"Bingham, it is time we had a talk. I don't want to waste any more time or effort on your flunkies. Just you and me. I'll be at the Ala Wai Lounge in one hour. I'd advise you to show up." Martin hung up before Bingham could answer. He hoped his voice had the right mixture of determination and desperation. He also wondered if one hour was too much time. Bingham could not be given time to plot a strategy. Keeping him off balance was essential.

Bingham was partly amused. He had always expected Martin to force a kind of show-down. It was all in the plan. You push your victim as far as possible, get him to make mistakes. Then when he cracks and demands a deal you have his good reputation in your pocket. Martin had gone well down that road. If he was ever to have a political future, thought Bingham, he would have to accept whatever Bingham was willing to offer. After all, Bingham already had enough dirt on the personal lifestyle angle. Coupled with Martin's questionable behavior and probably illegal tampering with official insurance records, there was little leverage the Senator had. A good stiff exchange of money would dig Bobby in even deeper. Bingham would meet with Martin alright, but it would be a meeting Martin would regret.

***

The Ala Wai Lounge was perfect for a private meeting. There were two entrances, and both went through a darkened hallway and reception area. The Lounge itself was a series of tall booths, well insulated from each other. A private meeting could be arranged easily without drawing attention to anyone coming and going.

It took Bingham several seconds to adjust his eyes to the dark interior. As he paused, he did not see the man waiting for him near the door. "You see that booth in the far corner?" Bingham recognized Martin's voice, trying to sound overdramatic, he thought. "You sit down and order a drink. I'll be along when I'm sure you came alone."

Martin let Bingham sit for fifteen minutes before he slid into the booth opposite him, his eyes glancing around the room the way he had seen it done in the movies. Bingham noticed Martin had a manila envelop. No doubt the incriminating evidence he would try to use as leverage, thought Bingham. As he slid into the dark booth his arm knocked over the beer bottle in Bingham's direction. "That's all right," came the irritated response as he dabbed up the puddled beer on the table top. The incident was sufficient to prevent Bingham from noticing a man gliding noiselessly into an adjacent booth.

Martin waited until the waitress came and returned with his order of scotch and water before he began. Bingham sat in amused silence.

Ramsey Bingham knew just how to flatter his opponents with the right amount of seriousness, often abruptly contrasted with playfulness or dismissal. Martin appeared unable to avoid looking at Bingham's almost ponderous face. It was a large face and large head. In photographs he looked more like an underworld figure than a chief executive officer for a major corporation. His bulging eyes trapped an unwilling victim.

His expression this day, born of confidence and experience in the art of manipulation, attempted to convey a gift to Martin. *Alright, Bobby, let's talk like the big boys talk*, it seemed to say. Martin's finger tightened ever so slightly on the envelop, giving him enough courage to ignore his own feelings of inferiority. In spite of his considerable self esteem, Bobby Martin, like so many men and women in public life, held a deep admiration for those among the species who moved with big ideas, big projects, and big money. Ramsey Bingham was the epitome of power in the private sector. After several years in the center of public decision making, most legislators began to realize, or imagine, that real power in their society was wielded by people like Bingham. The Binghams of the world allowed politicians to dabble in power, but when push came to shove. It was part of the magic and mystery of power. Business leaders, great or small, imagined the grand abuses of power and arrogance of the politician. Few actually had the courage to get to know them. When they did, their respect tended to decline, not so much as a result of the character of political leaders, but more as a by-product of their own values. They valued money and resources. Politicians valued fame and institutional controls. These were invisible. The world of the business tycoon was concrete. Each realm defended its own perspective. Each suffered a hidden yearning for the others.

"Our relationship is going to end today, Bingham," Martin began.

"I think you've been drinking a little too much, Bobby," Bingham searched his brain trying to anticipate what Martin could possibly know.

Martin removed a set of 8 X 10 black and white photographs from the envelope. He slapped them in front of Bingham and watched with bitter satisfaction Bingham slowly, almost reverently, leaf through them. They told the story of the cover-up of a chemical dump in a cane field, and the murder of one Bill Wilcox. Bingham's eyes focused on the limousine, the license number clearly visible. He began to realize there would be no difficulty in identifying it as one of his own. Of course, there was no visible evidence of his presence. But the other actors would be identified. Questions would be asked. It would take tremendous resources to construct enough alibis for all concerned. In the end the most he could hope for was a hung jury.

Bingham did not bother to look through the entire pile of pictures. He stared with burning rage at Bobby Martin as he carefully returned them to the envelope. He wondered who else had copies.

"These are impressive photos, Senator. These could get the owner into a lot of trouble. Where did you get these?"

Martin said nothing. He just stared expressionless into Bingham's large face. He knew it was up to Bingham to make the next move.

"Look, Martin, I know, and I have heard, that you've been through a lot. Perhaps I could make inquiries. Perhaps I could find out who has been hassling you. You know I have a lot of connections. I could be useful."

Martin continued to examine Bingham's face. He felt that gradually he was taking charge of the situation, without even having to say anything. It had a calming effect on him. It gave him confidence and patience. He could sit and wait for Bingham to unravel before his eyes. Bingham looked into Martin's eyes, hoping for a reaction. He found only an invitation to continue. He drained his glass of beer and ordered another. Martin had not touched his scotch.

"You've got to tell me what you want, Bobby," said Bingham with a new hint of familiarity. "Are you going to just sit there and wait for me to stumble across what you want? We both have better things to do than this. I won't kid you. Those are damning pictures. We both know it. So how are we going to resolve it, huh?" No reaction came from Bobby Martin. He remembered his instructions: *make sure Bingham is the one who suggests the deal. It has to be him, not you.*

"OK Martin," said Bingham with resignation in his voice. "I can make you a wealthy man. I can ensure you a brilliant career in politics. Next year is an election year, right? I can make sure your campaign coffers are full." No reaction. "I can extend that. The next election and the next. In fact, you want to be governor? I can do that. Don't look so surprised." Bobby Martin was not looking surprised, but Bingham was not really talking to him, more to himself. "I can mobilize tremendous amounts of support. Of course, there are limits. We can't do this overnight. Maybe not the next gubernatorial election, but the one after that…yeah, five years. That's enough time. I have no doubt, should you agree, that we can arrange for Governor Robert Martin's election." He peered into Martin's expression, searching for a telltale twitch of ambition. He found none.

Milking the moment for all it was worth, Martin deliberately took a small sip of his drink, cradling his glass as he would imagine George Smiley, the master English spy might do it. In fact, Martin was a great fan of Le Carre and he allowed himself to be transported into a more exotic setting, perhaps Istanbul or some such place. He allowed Ramsey Bingham to become a Russian double agent who had just been found out and could never go back to his people. A man who knew he had to cut a deal, now or never. Smiley would have to push his prey but not so far that he felt cornered. A cornered man might resort to violence. Not Smiley. He would handle it just right. So could Martin.

As if he had made up his mind, Bingham's attitude seemed to change. He no longer had the look of a beaten man. He reached into his suit coat pocket, a gesture that nearly scared the wits out of Martin, who half expected a gun to appear. Bingham withdrew a large stack of bills just as Carleton Brent had advised him to do in case Martin had anything incriminating to trade.

He was obviously taken aback by the hardheaded bargaining ability of Bobby Martin. *I always figured this Senator to be especially vulnerable to intimidation. He never suspected that he could be so cold and unmovable. Damn Wilcox. He had pushed this guy too far. He had turned him into a viper out for revenge. A lesson learned.* He allowed himself these thoughts because they distracted him from his true sense of panic. Bingham had always been the one in control. Now he was in deep trouble. He had taken an enormous risk. But he was sure, he told himself, that the secrecy of the meeting meant that Martin simply wanted out from under the blackmail. This was the tradeoff: Martin would get his payoff, and benefit politically to boot. If Bingham were not so frightened, he would have chuckled at how this wishy-washy politician had gotten the best of him.

Martin took a long swig of his drink, as if to indicate that the amount was adequate. But he said no words of agreement. Bingham was certain he had offered enough, although he was willing to double the amount on the spot. He had another pocket full, if necessary, plus stock options on Sandwich Isle Chemical. That was the last resort.

Whispering, Bingham said, "I think we have an understanding now Martin. I expect to receive in the mail the negatives within one week, then the remaining payments will follow. You don't have to say anything more. I understand. This is not the kind of thing you do everyday. But remember this. If you ever go back on this deal you can kiss off your life and that of your family's. Ramsey Bingham plays for keeps." Bingham picked up the envelope, gently nudged the pile of bills toward Bobby Martin, stood up, and walked toward the door.

Martin watched passively as the shadow of Ramsey Bingham in the door frame was met by two plain clothes detectives. Bingham raised his voice in protest. The man in the next booth slipped out and glanced at martin. Bobby nodded soberly to Byron Park who scooped up the dirty money and quickly strode to the door and took charge of the arrest.

***

Michael Robinson always had a special relationship with Mei-ling Bridges. In spite of the friction between Michael and Eastland, their social circles were intermixed. It was so often the case in Hawaii. The Islands were a cluster of minorities and networks. This community, Mei-ling reflected, was so much like society in Asia, where clans and extended families created small groups for survival and competing allegiance.

Yet Hawaii was different, too. Not only was everyone in a minority, but society was also overlaid with dozens and dozens of intense multiethnic social groups: from alumni of the same high school, to members of the same union, to members of the same army battalion, to loyalists of the first democratic governor...on and on.

The net result, felt Mei-ling, was a continuing sense of intimacy. Rumors and gossip were constant. Not so different from any small town or village, she thought. And yet, Honolulu was hardly a small town. It was cosmopolitan. It was one of the major cities of the United States, eleventh by population. Because of the tourist industry, the quality and quantity of live entertainment was far above that of comparable urban centers on the mainland. It was, like so many growing and modern urban centers, choked with rush-hour traffic and hard up for affordable housing. Yet there was this intimacy.

Michael Robinson used to say that residents of Hawaii cared less about politics than their cousins on the mainland, but actually knew more. Politics was interwoven with daily gossip. So and so's auntie worked for a senator who was married to your brother's classmate. That councilmember went to school with your insurance salesman. It was a place where hardly anything about the near-famous could remain a secret. A public figure had to be constantly on the alert to pick up on damaging rumors and innuendo.

In such a place, people like Michael Robinson and Mei-ling Bridges, united by past affiliations, divided by recent disagreements, found uneasy, but sustainable relationships. They could always talk to, if not trust, each other. They maintained a continued interest in following each other's ups and downs. When Mei-ling telephoned Michael, it was in this tradition of island civility that he agreed to meet. Helen knew that Michael could never refuse Mei-ling Bridges.

At the very moment that Helen was driving to Kapiolani Park for her meeting with Brent, Mei-ling was sitting next to the tall curtained windows which looked out on the parking lot of the Ala Moana Restaurant. It was part of a department store, yet separate enough to provide a relaxed, almost colonial atmosphere. The early evening hour was just late enough to avoid the shoppers, and just early enough before the rush of diners. She sipped her tea with an elegance and grace while thinking of Helen, and waiting for Michael.

When Michael arrived he was again captivated by her charm and beauty. Twenty years his senior, she dominated their corner of the restaurant with her femininity. *Here was a lady I was born too late for*, he thought. She acknowledged his arrival, and extended her hand to his, as he sat down and apologized for his tardiness, which both knew was calculated. As he chatted about the laziness and beauty of the late afternoon, she observed his new premature gray on his temples, and marveled at how he had changed from his days as a staffer in her husband's office. He knew she was inspecting him, and he enjoyed her attentions.

"It was nice of you to come, Michael. I've hardly seen you since you began to be such a successful politician. But I always knew you would do well."

"My pleasure, Mei-ling. I'm sorry I wasn't able to attend your last Christmas party. We young legislators tend to get all caught up in our own work, I'm afraid. But I'm glad you called. I got the impression that you had something on your mind, something you wanted to talk about?"

How like Michael to leap abruptly from social graces to business. Not at all like Eastland, who somehow had learned the fine art of conversation and subtlety. I wonder if such talents are dying out altogether with this new generation.

"Yes, it was very perceptive of you. In fact, I must tell you how impressed I have been with your abilities. Right from those articles the paper ran on you as a freshman up to now, you seem to be in the limelight. And always so certain and well spoken. I know you and Eastland did not see eye to eye, but I always felt his first staff, you, Helen, Betsy, were part of his, our family. For that reason, I hope you don't feel offended when I tell you that I am proud of you. Proud of one of *us* doing well."

Michael was both flattered and uneasy. He had been around Mei-ling Bridges just long enough to knew when she as playing out a ritual, setting him up psychologically for serious business. "And you wanted to see me?" he reminded.

"Michael, what I am going to say, what I am going to ask is not easy for me. It has not been a kind year. Eastland was so much a part of my life. His passing has left me without a purpose. I know that eventually I will have to start off on a new path alone. But before I can do that I must settle my own accounts with Eastland. I must know the circumstances of his death."

"I guess you know as much as I do. The police are convinced…"

"Michael, I am begging you to tell me what you know. For an old friend, and I hope we are still friends, for a foolish widow, please…"

"Mei-ling, I think you are expecting more than I can give. I'm as much in the dark as you," he answered, aware that the blood was beginning to drain from his head. Mei-ling seemed to know more than he expected.

She looked at Michael with great disappointment. Her sadness was not for the young man on the make that sat before her as much for the Hawaii she had come to love and call her home. He was the new breed, a small but growing group who had been nurtured in the shadow of government and elevated too soon, in her view. He did not represent the majority of new politicians, most of whom were idealistic and impatient for change. He was one of the patient, practical ones. One of those who go along for years, biding their time to achieve power, and then when it arrives, unable to remember what it was that drove them to it. *Heaven help us from the patient young ones*, she thought. *They were more likely to sell out.*

With a stiffened resolve that Michael could feel across the table, she carefully removed several notes from her purse. One by one she laid them on the table in front of Michael so he could read them. He read each one, hoping somehow the contents would change before his eyes so he would not have to explain. They were two of the three letters sent by Bill Wilcox to the wrong people. One intended for Michael, but sent to Betsy. One intended for Betsy, but sent to Bobby Martin, resulting in what must have been high comedy, if it weren't so fatal. *What a rotten combination of bad luck*, thought Michael, *that this particular underling Wilcox would make such a mistake, and would have the curious habit of addressing and signing notes with a capital letter rather than a full name: "Dear B…"* No wonder Martin flipped out. He knew their content without reading, but he read slowly to buy time, to think of what to say. It did no good. His composure was leaving and taking his ability to think on his feet with it. He looked up at Mei-ling, who waited patiently but stubbornly for an explanation.

"No need to explain all the circumstance, Michael. To tell you the truth, I don't want to know what they all mean. I did not want to have to resort to this, but I am willing to do anything, anything Michael, to honor my husband. I must know what to tell his child. We must be able to close the book on his life with honor and completeness. You must tell me what happened."

Michael took a sip of coffee without looking at her. He was thinking that perhaps it would do no harm to reveal the circumstance of Eastland's death. Mei-ling was a grieving widow. She wanted simply the whole story, and then she would pack up with her kid and go off to the family in Hong Kong, never to appear again in Michael's life. Perhaps he owed her this one. Perhaps this was his way of returning the dignified encouragement she had once given him.

"Eastland's death was a complete accident," he began as his eyes and fingers focused on the spoon in front of him. It was easier not to look at her directly. "And he did not fall down as a result of drinking too much pineapple wine." He looked up, expecting to find Mei-ling relieved, but she was not. Her expression never changed, because she had never accepted the story of his intoxication.

"Eastland did not fall, he was pushed. You see, he had in his files some very important papers. What they were is that …they, they, would have affected my clients, and pending legislation. I needed to get them. But I feared that Eastland would not agree, and besides, he was going off on a trip and we could not wait until he returned," he lied. Mei-ling seemed to know what parts was truth and what parts fabricated to save face. She tolerated his slightly tailored versions. He was glad she did not press the point.

"We sent Bill Wilcox, our foreman, to borrow the files. He was able to get a key from Betsy, you know they were close, and delivered a case of pineapple wine in the process. Bill had not had an easy life, and apparently he sat in Eastland's office and drank a whole bottle of wine. Eastland unexpectedly stopped in the office, I guess before going to the airport, and confronted Bill going through his files, drunk as hell, pardon the expression. Startled and frightened, Wilcox pushed Eastland out of the way and ran out of the office. He didn't know or remember exactly what happened, but the best we can figure out is when he pushed Eastland he hit his head on the corner of the desk." Try as he might, Michael could not tell his story without emotion. Eastland Bridges was his mentor, at least at first, and he had been distraught for days when learning that his scheme to steal papers on chemical pollution had resulted in the accidental death of a future leader of Hawaii.

Michael Robinson, for all his compromises, was not beyond guilt or remorse. As he sat before Mei-ling Bridges, he was filled with tragedy, for Bridges and for himself. His fancy plans had backfired. People had died. He had allowed himself to become involved in blackmail, theft, and the cover-up of a crime. And now he was sitting in front of a widow, a lady he had partly caused to become a widow, and he suddenly felt terrible. His youth could not insulate him from his sense of self betrayal. Mei-ling saw this but said nothing.

With moisture in his eyes and frog in his throat, Michael told his confessor his journey from aspiring politician on the make to his first compromise with Ramsey Bingham. He explained his exhilaration at dealing with the powerful men of Hawaii, of being in on big business and big deals. He tried to communicate to her how exciting it was for such a young person to be welcomed into the inner world of land deals, and to be confided in. His new found connections with Bingham opened doors at the legislature, and more campaign funds than he could use. He played the game with zest, he confessed. But he never, never expected it would really hurt anyone. He was not a bad person. She must understand. She must find some way to forgive him for what had happened to her husband. A horrible accident, to be sure. But he was not a criminal. They were just business men who found themselves painted into a corner and went too far to get out. Life was filled with such tragedies. Surely she could understand. Surely she could forgive him.

"So Eastland was…Eastland died because someone wanted his files." She interpreted, not without emotion in her voice. "Would it be safe to say those files were part of his legislative work, that he found something important to the community?" she asked.

"Very important, Mei-ling. You see Eastland was about to uncover the fact that Sandwich Isle Chemical had been dumping chemicals in an abandoned cane filed. Technically, it was illegal. But you know those environmentalists, always passing laws too strict. We figured it would do no harm. But then things started leaking out, so to speak. These guys are not crooks, you know. They are just smart businessmen trying to maximize their profits. After all, profits are the bottom line."

"Yes, Michael. Today profits are the bottom line," she echoed, somewhat distant from him. "Did Eastland find out about Mrs. Garcia? Was he trying to help her?"

"No doubt. Sure, he would have helped this one woman. We were not against helping her. But it had to be done quietly. We were under pressure form our insurance people." Michael was speaking faster now, trying to find in his justification comfort for himself and reasons for Mei-ling not to be bitter against him. He rambled on, not really speaking with conviction, mostly repeating the hundreds of conversations he had had with the Ramsey Binghams and Bill Wilcoxes. The rationalizations. The bottom lines.

"So now you know the whole story. I'm glad it's finally over," said Michael, drained and weakened.

"Not quite over, Mr. Robinson."

Michael glanced up and found himself in the shadow of a stern-faced man looking directly down at him. It was a face he instantly recognized. It was the final blow.

"Thank you Mrs. Bridges," said Byron Park. Silently, without looking directly at Michael, Mei-ling opened her purse and handed

Detective Park the small tape recorder. Michael stared in disbelief as she rose and walked from the room. He hung his head in despair as Park led him out into the early evening dusk to the patrol car.

"Park here," answered the detective into his car intercom.

"We missed them. They checked out of the hotel about forty-five minutes ago. Headed for the airport, they said," squawked the voice on the other end.

"Roger." Byron Park was afraid he would be too late. He gunned the engine and headed for Kapiolani Park, calling for backup support. It was just like Helen Tokugawa to get herself into this kind of a mess, he muttered. It was only by accident that Mei-ling happened to mention Helen's meeting with Brent. Park was able to badger her into revealing their scheme, but only after warning that the meeting could be dangerous for Helen. He could feel the sweat on his brow as he got stuck in traffic on his way into Waikiki.

The shadows grew longer and then disappeared altogether as the park grew gloomy around Helen. She glanced nervously at her watch, and rechecked the small tape recorder in her purse. Surely Brent would show up, she reasoned. After all, Stephani had played her role well. This was Helen's chance to strike a blow for exploited women everywhere, and in the meantime collect some incriminating evidence of conspiracy.

She noticed a limousine glide to a halt off to her left, between her and the beach park. The musicians on the fringe of the park pounded on their syncopated bongos, providing just the right atmosphere of intrigue, she felt. A man in a suit exited the limo, carrying a black briefcase. He oriented himself, then began walking deliberately towards the bandstand. Soon he was able to make out Helen sitting on the benches. He adjusted his pathway, sure that this was the woman who insisted on meeting. The man in the trees behind Helen quietly emerged and moved swiftly towards Helen's back.

In spite of all her planning, Helen's heart began to pound, her hands grew sweaty. She rose as the well-groomed Englishman approached. She could smell his cologne.

"You, I presume, are Julia?"

"And you are Carleton…" a large hand slapped her mouth shut as she was pulled to the ground. Before she could speak or scream a gag was forced on her and tied roughly by Brent's associate. Brent looked nonchalantly to make sure there were no observers. Helen's eyes bugged when she saw the man remove a knife from his pocket. He pushed the button and the blade snapped out: shlick.

"Freeze" came an angry voice off to the right. Brent turned and began to run. The blond man jerked his head just as the officer's gun erupted. The wounded killer lurched back towards the trees, this time armed with a large automatic silencer. Spit... spit. An officer was down. The large man turned to run when the shotgun blast exploded into his chest.

POSTSCRIPT

"*The trials of former State Representative Michael Robinson and business tycoons Ramsey Bingham and Carleton Brent are finally over. Guilty on two counts of conspiracy to suppress evidence for Robinson, was the verdict of the five women, seven-man jury. Bingham and Brent were found guilty of more serious crimes, conspiracy to commit murder and blackmail.*

"Prosecutor Henry Goto was quoted as saying that the trials closed the books on one of the most complicated and political of crimes in the history of Hawaii. Asked if there were any more indictments to come, Goto responded, "I hope not. This community has been through enough."

"Indeed, it has been nearly two years since KARE TV first broke the story of the cane field cover-up. Since then, Hawaii has gone through a major election campaign where literally dozens of races were decided based on how voters felt about this case. For the most part, voters stood firmly with those in the State Senate who had been closest to the late Senator Eastland Bridges."

"Senator Robert Martin, the victim of blackmail because of his personal life, testified at the trial in an emotional display of courage which apparently did much to ensure his overwhelming re-election."

"Tomorrow, we begin a special five-part report on the impact of this case on the personal lives of those most affected, from the famous to the obscure."

"Until then, this is Barbara Lum reporting live from Circuit court for KARE NEWS."

Randall Ogawa snapped off the television and walked briskly to the bathroom to make sure his hair was just right. He felt a slight twitch of discomfort in his ribs as he sat down to wait another twenty minutes. He thought of that evening two years ago when he and Helen had been talking about children, and how their enjoyment in being with each other had ended with unexpected violence. Helen was a terrific woman, he reflected. Perhaps if I hadn't been so full of adventure, she wouldn't have gotten into so much trouble on her own. Randall was not a little guilty over being laid up in the hospital at the very moment Helen had needed him. He shuddered to think again of the tall killer that stalked them without their knowledge. There was a rap on the door.

"Yeah?"

"We're ready for you Randy. Do you have the…"

"Got it," he answered, slapping his front pocket for assurance.

He slipped on his tuxedo, adjusted his tie, and left the private room near the altar to enter the church. His nose was filled with smell of lilies. Helen's favorite, he smiled to himself. He joined his best man Bobby Martin and waited for his future wife, Helen Tokugawa, to march down the isle.